"So you married me to punish me, Yves?"

With great effort, Marianne kept the shock from her voice and hoped her face showed nothing of her inner turmoil. "I don't have to stay here, you know."

"Oh, no, Marianne." Yves's gray eyes glittered at her. "You won't leave. You like some parts of being married—very much." His gaze swept boldly over her, and her swift rise of color told him he was indeed right.

"You like being married sometimes, too!" Marianne flung back. "As for punishing me . . . you don't seem to be having much success. Perhaps you'd better try harder—"

"You tempt me, dear wife," he whispered seductively.

As he reached for her Marianne trembled, knowing he touched her with desire, never love, the worst hurt of all. . . .

Harlequin Premiere Editions

1—**MORE THAN YESTERDAY** by Jeneth Murrey
2—**THE LION'S DEN** by Ann Cooper
3—**THE RUAIG INHERITANCE** by Jean S. MacLeod
4—**THE WILLING HEART** by Helen Bianchin
5—**THE STORM EAGLE** by Lucy Gillen
6—**THE KURRANULLA ROUND** by Dorothy Cork
7—**BELOVED SURGEON** by Sheila Douglas
8—**FLASH OF EMERALD** by Jane Arbor
9—**AT THE VILLA ROMANA** by Anne Vinton
10—**AUTUMN IN BANGKOK** by Jacqueline Gilbert
11—**PIRATE LOVER** by Margaret Mayo
12—**FORESTS OF THE DRAGON** by Rosemary Carter

Harlequin Books

TORONTO • LONDON • LOS ANGELES • AMSTERDAM
SYDNEY • HAMBURG • PARIS • STOCKHOLM • ATHENS • TOKYO

Original hardcover edition published in 1981
by Mills & Boon Limited

ISBN 0-373-82101-8

This Harlequin Premiere Editions volume
published October 1981

Printed in U.S.A.

CHAPTER ONE

MARIANNE smoothed the creases out of the telegram and read it again.

'I *must* go,' she said stubbornly, and the words were full of a desperate determination.

Liz Ross surveyed her friend with sardonic blue eyes while she arranged herself more comfortably in the big armchair.

'What's so pressing?' she demanded. 'You get a telegram from someone you haven't seen for eight years and you drop everything. You throw up your job and start flinging things in suitcases! Why don't you sit down quietly, count up to ten and tell little Liz all about it?'

'Grand'mère is ill, probably dying. I *have* to go!' Even to herself, Marianne sounded obstinate, and she lowered her head to re-read the two letters she had just finished writing.

'All right,' Liz waved an airy hand, 'so there's some urgency, but the old lady's not a real relation, she only brought you up—or so you told me. I remember quite well. Your parents were killed in a car smash somewhere in France and this Frenchwoman took you in. Very romantic!'

'It wasn't romantic at all.' Marianne let herself slide back in time. 'I was about seven and the only survivor. The rescue party took me to Grand'mère at La Barrière—that's the name of the farm; and as you just said, she took me in.'

'It would have been much more romantic if it had been a chateau and if the old lady had been a duchess.' Liz cocked an impertinent blue eye. 'Farms and farmers' wives sound so earthy. Didn't you have any guardians or trustees to look after you?'

'There wasn't anybody except old Mr Gillespie, Daddy's solicitor, and he didn't know what to do with me.' Marianne's mouth curved into a wry smile. 'He came to France to see me and to tell Grand'mère that he had arranged a place for me at a boarding school.' She chuckled at that far-away memory. 'Grand'mère wiped the floor with him, especially when he started talking about compensation for her trouble. She told him that *she* would care for me if a boarding school was the best he could arrange and he could save my money for a *dot*—that's a French girl's marriage portion. Anyway, Mr Gillespie scuttled back to England and left me with Grand'mère. I think I embarrassed him.'

'But why go back now?' Liz returned to the attack like a terrier at a rathole. 'You've been here in London for eight years and you've never once gone back before—and don't tell me that you're expecting to inherit something, because I know you better than that and you've got plenty of money anyway.'

'You make me sound like a millionairess,' protested Marianne, 'and I'm no such thing! The money my parents left plus what old Mr Gillespie got for the house and things just sat in banks and deposits for ten years and grew. It wouldn't be enough to live on, not nowadays.'

Marianne remembered the lovely times in those ten years at La Barrière, the woman she had called Grand'mère and the warmth and safety of those black-clad arms and bosom. It didn't take long for a child to settle down, especially when the child was made welcome and given all the love she could want. Within the space of six short months, Mary Anne Montgomery had become Marianne Montgomerie and as French as a bottle of Beaujolais!

'Wasn't there a grandson?' Liz broke in on her reverie and Marianne felt a sharp stab of pain. She looked at her friend and Liz returned the look with wide, innocent blue eyes. 'I remember you saying that he married just before you left and then, about four years ago, you said that his wife had died. Has he married again?'

'Looking for more romance, Liz?' Marianne made it sound light and inconsequential, and deliberately turned back to her letters so that Liz should not see her face. In the long mirror on the lounge wall she caught a glimpse of herself. Taller than average, slim and graceful with long, slender legs and narrow feet and hands. Her long, marmalade-coloured hair was brushed into a smooth chignon and her hazel eyes, in their fringe of dark lashes, were clear and peaceful. Her face was a smooth, pale oval with a small, straight nose and a too-wide mouth; an expressionless oval, she noted with satisfaction. She had trained herself to that calm, competent look when she had been in the secretarial college and it was now second nature to her to wear it.

'That's your Madonna look!' Liz was tart. 'You always wear it when you're hiding something. Although, with that colour hair, you're not a Madonna, you're a Magdalene! I want to know what's going on—I think I'll come with you.'

'No need.' Marianne hunted in the drawer for stamps. 'I'll write to you as soon as I know what I'm going to do and if I'm not back by Christmas you can call on your way to Switzerland.'

'Ahah!' Liz's eyes snapped. 'You're up to something! It's the grandson, isn't it? If he hasn't remarried, you're going after him. Don't bother to deny it. I always knew there was a man somewhere, and you just don't want me along cramping your style.' She struggled to her feet and made for the door. 'I'll go and make myself useful, shall I? I'll check your Mini.'

'What would I do without you?' Marianne smiled at the petite blonde.

'Pay out a fortune in garage bills,' Liz grinned back.

'Don't get maudlin, ducky. I know I'm not all that I should be, but I'm a dab hand with a spanner!'

When she had gone, Marianne re-read her letters. One to her boss, a big man in a big oil company who would miss his super-efficient secretary; she hoped he would understand. The other was to her bank manager, asking him to make funds available to her at the Crédit Lyonnais in Rémy. She checked through her bag, her passport was in order and the booklet of travellers' cheques was tucked safely inside it. Her mind went leaping ahead. She would have to buy a few francs on the boat. Not many, just enough for travelling expenses down to La Barrière.

'Anything to eat?' Liz yelled from the front door of the flat they shared.

'Omelettes!' Marianne sealed up her letters before going into the ultra-modern kitchen to beat eggs while she thought about La Barrière and Grand'mère. Her movements were quick and neat as she prepared the evening meal and laid the small table in the dining area. She diced cold chicken to make a filling for the omelettes and brought a lemon cheesecake from the fridge.

'Nothing wrong at all.' Liz came in and seated herself. 'That Mini of yours could go to Hongkong and back, never mind the middle of France. The tourist rush is over, so you should have a quiet crossing. I still think I should come with you,' she worried aloud. 'What's he like, the grandson?'

The abrupt question caught Marianne off guard so that her mouth curved into a smile before she could do anything to stop it. Hastily she pulled herself together.

'He was very nice,' she murmured in a colourless voice, and Liz gave a grunt of disgust.

'Tall, short, dark, fair? "Very nice" can mean almost anything. Has he remarried? Does he squint or talk with a lisp?'

Marianne chased crumbs of cheesecake around her

plate while she thought how best to describe Yves. 'Tall,' she peered back into her memory. 'About six foot, I think. Dark, black hair and a sort of olive complexion, grey eyes, slim, a thin, clever face—and kind. He was always very kind to me when I was a little girl.'

'I'd make a wonderful Indentikit picture out of that!' Liz jeered.

'It's eight years since I saw him last,' Marianne protested. 'I don't think he's remarried—Grand'mère would have mentioned it, I feel sure.'

Liz reached a small, square, competent hand across the table and covered Marianne's long fingers in a warm clasp. 'I won't tease any more. Go back, Marianne. Go on your little pilgrimage to yesterday, and if the going gets a bit rough for you, give me a call and I'll come and lend you a hand over the hard bits. A repayment for the times when you've helped me over *my* hard bits. Meanwhile, I shall go and check your oil, brakes and steering while you throw a few more things in your suitcase.'

As Liz had predicted, the cross-Channel ferries were half empty and the sea was as calm as a millpond. It was nearly the end of September and the tourist rush was over. Marianne saw her Mini tucked in on the car deck and went to stand at the stern, watching the propellers churn the green water into a creamy foam with a feeling of relief. She was going home.

After she had skirted Paris, she drove down the N7 to Clermont-Ferrand and about fifty miles farther on, she turned left on to a winding road that snaked its way south of the Puy de Dome down to Cahors. At the little town of Rémy she took the small country road to Serac Ste Marie and at Serac turned the nose of the Mini up the hill road that led only to the farm called La Barrière.

It was early evening when she arrived and she drew the Mini to a halt in the cobbled farmyard just outside the kitchen door. She was tired and sticky and her shoulders were aching with the strain of driving. Wearily she clambered out of the car and went to the door, her hand raised to clasp the knocker.

Before she could do anything, the door swung open and Marianne looked up into the face of the man who stood there watching her. It was Yves; she would have known him if she had been blindfold, she didn't need eyes to tell him from any other man in the world—but this wasn't the Yves she had known. She dredged up her memories of Yves and saw him once again smiling down at her in the sunlight. Tall and slim, his black hair falling over his forehead and his thin, sensitive face alight with humour and understanding.

This Yves was tall, but there all similarity ended. Eight years had broadened him so that he was now a big man, his black hair still fell forward, but there was silver in it now and it was worn longer than she had remembered it; it curled slightly against his collar—but it was his face that made her heart cringe. It was a mask of cold impassivity with only the eyes alive in it and there was nothing warm or gentle in those steel-grey slits under his heavy lids. They were full of an insolent evaluation, a bitter mockery, and he looked at her with a cold, derisive calculation which she had never met before.

Marianne blinked and let her face set in the cool, competent lines into which it had been trained and she spoke in her quiet, impersonal voice.

'Good evening, Yves. I'm not too late?'

'She said that you would be coming, I did not think so.' His head jerked to signify the sick woman upstairs. 'She said that she would wait for you.' There was no welcome in his voice, no interest even, he had summed her up and dismissed her as being not worth his trouble. Marianne stepped around him and went past him and out of the door on the farther side of the kitchen. He followed her to the bottom of the stairs and his harsh voice floated up the stairs after her. 'She has been waiting for three days. Now perhaps she will allow herself to die.'

Grand'mère looked grey and shrunken in the wide white bed and there was an urgency in the clasp of the birdlike claw of her hand. For a while she lay there quietly as if recruiting her strength, her eyes closed and the old hand lax in Marianne's grasp, then the hand stirred and Grand'mère opened her dark eyes.

'I have been wicked, *ma petite fille*, and it is for you to put it right. It is too late for me.' The clawlike fingers tightened. 'Once before I tried to play God and now again I have done it. But you will put it right—promise?'

'I promise.'

Marianne knelt, holding the old hand, until Yves came and lifted her away from the bed and drew the sheet up over the stern, dead face. She looked at him with wonder, this remote, cold Yves with the bitter eyes and the hard cruel mouth. This was an Yves she did not know, did not want to know. He carried her down to the kitchen and sat her in the sagging cane rocker by the fire.

'Little fool! Why did you not call? Kneeling by a dead woman for over an hour!'

'I didn't know that she was dead.' Marianne accepted the cup of coffee he pushed into her fingers. 'I thought that she was asleep, that now her mind was at rest, perhaps she would get better.'

He looked his contempt at her. But it was different for him, she told herself as she sipped the coffee. Yves was a farmer, he had trained as a vet. He saw death and life every day, they were no strangers to him. She had never seen anyone dead in her life except her parents, and that was too long ago. Time had wiped out that memory.

'I will take you down to the *auberge* in the village.' He reached for a sheepskin jacket hung on a hook by the back door. 'They will find a room for you until the funeral.'

'No!' Marianne shook her head. 'I'll stay here.'

He shrugged. 'As you wish, mademoiselle. I will bring up one of the women from the village to do what is needful. It will not worry you to stay here with a dead woman upstairs? I shall have to deprive you of my company, of course.' He made it sound like an insult. 'This is provincial France, mademoiselle. You have not forgotten our code of morals, have you?' The sneer was thick on his tongue. 'The *curé* will give me a bed and your reputation will be safe.' He shrugged on his jacket and the door slammed behind him.

Marianne heard the engine of a car start into life and through the uncurtained window watched the headlights swing round to point downhill. She was too tired to wait for whoever was coming from the village. In Yves's bedroom, she stripped the sheets from his bed and undressing down to her slip, slid between the blankets, reflecting grimly that it was as well that she had stopped in Clermont-Ferrand for a meal. There was no welcome for her here at La Barrière.

She would stay, though, Grand'mère had asked her to come and had extracted that promise to put something right. What it was, she didn't know. It didn't matter anyway. Tomorrow, she mused as she drifted off to sleep.

For the next three days, Marianne lived in the kitchen and in Yves's bedroom. There were a great many other rooms in the old house, but she did not venture into any of them. There were memories there which were better left sleeping. The coffin had been taken down to the little church in Serac Ste. Marie and the funeral would be on Thursday. That was tomorrow, she realised with a start of surprise. The days had gone past swiftly, but there had been a lot to do; there was still a lot to do.

Grandmère's chickens were fed as they had not been fed since the old lady had taken to her bed, and Marianne hunted around in hedges and in long tussocks of grass for those eggs which had been laid away. She also scrubbed every piece of the kitchen that was scrubbable, so that on the day of the funeral she awaited Yves, Monsieur Julot, the notary, Tante Monique and Bernard in a spick and span kitchen, a kitchen of which Grand'mère would not have been ashamed.

The fire in the big wood-burning range was low and Marianne chose small logs from the box to coax it back into life. She shifted the coffee pot across so that it would heat more quickly and set the cups and saucers on the table. Then, reluctantly, she went through to the salon to fetch the bottle of cognac and glasses from the cabinet where they were kept. It was cold in there and she shivered, cold and damp as though the room had not been used since that dreadful day, eight years ago, when Madame Fabré had brought her daughter Gisèle up to La Barrière and into this room. It felt as though all the bitterness, hate and misery were still here in the air. Marianne remembered Grand'mère's stern face as she had asked Yves, 'Could the child be yours?' and Yves's almost surly, 'Yes!'

Gisèle had been crying pathetically while Grand'mère and Madame Fabré had made the arrangements for the wedding. Yves had stood silent by the window and she, Marianne, had watched them all while her heart had broken painfully. She had seen the triumph naked on Madame Fabré's face and the sly pleasure that had lurked behind Gisèle's tears, for the farm and the vineyards of La Barrière were the biggest in the locality and Yves was a wealthy young man, or would be when Grand'mère died. A nice prize to fall into Gisèle's plump, grasping little hands!

Marianne had seen the displeasure on Grand'mère's face, felt the outrage in the black-clad old lady, and she had seen Yves. It was then that he had grown into the bitter, cold man! How stupid of her not to remember that! He had stood there like some trapped animal, waiting for Grand'mère's judgement, and Grand'mère had been harsh.

Yves would marry Gisèle or leave La Barrière; the choice was his, but it was no choice at all. Yves loved La Barrière, it was his life. From that moment all the love and warmth of La Barrière had died, and with it had died the Yves that Marianne had known.

Within a month of the marriage, everyone in Serac Ste. Marie knew that there had been a mistake. There would be no baby, there never had been a baby. Grand'mère's face had grown old and grey and Yves had looked at the old lady with bitter dead eyes. Gisèle had screamed in tantrums, complaining of poverty and neglect, while Yves worked from dawn till dusk and came in, morose and silent, to lock himself in the room which he called his office.

Meanwhile, Grand'mère kept up an unceasing monologue. Yves should take Gisèle to his bed. If there was no child this time, perhaps next time . . . And Yves had refused coldly and with an insolent twist to his mouth.

It was about at this time when Bernard became a frequent visitor at La Barrière: Yves's cousin, a younger, shorter, thicker man with hot black eyes and warm, damp hands. Marianne disliked him, his eyes were always on her long coltish legs and her young bosom and his hands seemed always to be touching her. Then, one day, Grand'mère had said 'Go' and Marianne had gone, to London to a secretarial college and a life vastly different from the provincial farmhouse in the shadow of the Puy de Dome.

The noise of a car coming up the hill brought Marianne back to the present and with cold, shaking hands she gathered up the cognac and glasses and went back to the kitchen. The funeral was over and Yves was bringing old Monsieur Julot back to the house, and with them would come Bernard and his mother Tante Monique. That was all the family that Yves had, and Tante would insist on coming just in case Grand'mère had decided to leave her something. Marianne pushed the coffee pot over the flames and fetched a jug of cream from the pantry, then went to the window to watch Yves's aged and impeccable Citroën pull into the farmyard. It was the first and only car he had ever bought and it looked as good now as it did when he had brought it home fourteen years ago.

Yves stood back and let his passengers precede him into the kitchen. Monsieur Julot came first, briefcase in hand, then came Tante Monique who glanced possessively around the room, followed by Bernard, whose round, boyish features were composed in an expression of grief which was at variance with the hot glow in his dark eyes. Marianne could almost read Tante's mind, what she would keep, what she would throw away. The sagging cane chair evoked a grimace of distaste on Tante's heavy features and Marianne found herself gripping the arms until her knuckles were white.

Bernard and his mother looked so confident, so sure of themselves! Her glance drifted across to Yves, trying to make out what he was thinking, but his dark face was enigmatic. He slouched in his chair, the white of his shirt making his skin look very dark, his eyes beneath their hooded lids seemed to glitter with a savage appreciation of Tante's gloved hands arranging the cups and saucers to her own satisfaction and her sideways sniff at the cream jug to assure herself that the contents were fresh.

Monsieur Julot shuffled papers from his briefcase and balanced his pince-nez on his nose while his dry little cough signalled that he was ready to begin. As he opened his mouth, Tante cut across in a flat, harsh voice.

'Mademoiselle Marianne, I do not think we need you.' There was a hard smile for the old notary. 'It is a family matter, is it not? And the girl is not of the family.'

'But she must stay.' The notary's voice, old like the rustle of dry leaves, was hesitant and Marianne smiled to herself. Monsieur Julot was afraid of Tante Monique, which wasn't surprising; most people were. Tante had all the tact and finesse of a runaway steamroller and she was accustomed to talking down opposition. As soon as she had started to object, Marianne had risen and was on her way to the door, but she halted as Yves moved in his chair.

'Sit down, *mademoiselle.*' His eyes met Marianne's with a savage satisfaction before he turned back to the old notary. 'My grandmother counted this English girl as one of the family and sent for her especially.'

Monsieur Julot nodded. 'She is mentioned,' he quavered, avoiding Tante's flushed face.

Marianne felt no particular satisfaction. This bit of byplay was Yves putting Tante in her place. Unhurriedly, she walked back to the cane rocker, her high heels clicking on the floor tiles.

Monsieur Julot seemed to think that sufficient time had been wasted, for he gabbled through the papers before him. Madame Victorine Bersac had been forthright and explicit, and her will was simple. La Barrière and everything upon it, together with a small fortune in cash and securities, was left jointly to her grandson Yves and Mademoiselle Mary Anne Montgomery with the proviso that they should marry within three months. If they did not, then it all became the property of her great-nephew, Bernard Fortin.

Tante Monique flushed with pleasure and Marianne frowned. So this was what Grand'mère had meant she had said that she was playing God! She cast a quick glance at Yves. His face was dark and withdrawn, only his eyes were alive, and a little tic at the corner of his mouth. Marianne heard Tante's flat, harsh voice.

'So, it is settled. What girl, even this English one, would marry such as him?' Tante's neat black toque jerked at Yves. 'What girl would take a chance with one of so uncertain a temper, such black, bitter moods? Gisèle paid dearly for her folly at his hands.' Tante folded her black-gloved hands and nodded to herself. 'Madame Bersac asked the impossible!' Other words were trembling on her lips and Marianne saw the heightened colour that betokened something better left unsaid. Tante Monique was choking back comments, she had said too much already.

'Not of me.' Marianne heard her own voice, clear and quiet, the words dropping separately into the silence. She was surprised at the steadiness of it. She saw Yves's black head turn towards her, but there was no softening of his features, only an insolent appraisal that made her feel sick inside.

'You agree to this?' Even Monsieur Julot seemed taken aback.

She found herself smiling into Tante's angry eyes, a gentle smile with no satisfaction in it, and out of the corner of her eye she watched Bernard. His hot little eyes now looked like flat, wet pebbles.

'I agree,' she said firmly, allowing no hesitation to cloud her words. 'It is what Grand'mère wished or she would not have written it so.' She gave the ghost of a Gallic shrug. 'That is one party to the agreement, is it not? The rest is for Monsieur Bersac to decide.'

She turned a calm, composed face to the notary while her thoughts sped on. Grand'mère had been wrong to do this. Hadn't the old lady seen the change in Yves? Hadn't she noticed that the young, happy, goodhumoured Yves was no longer there, that his place had been taken by this jeering, inscrutable man who seemed to hate everybody? 'Please, God,' she prayed silently, 'don't let him refuse. Make him take time to think.'

'It is a grave matter. We will have coffee now and some cognac, I think. It will warm us, and then later Mademoiselle Marianne and I will talk of this privately.' He turned back to the window to watch the raindrops, now streaking down the panes. Marianne sighed. Beneath the smooth words was an enjoyment at Tante's discomfiture, a hating! And it wasn't just Tante that was to suffer. Bernard would have his share and she, Marianne, was to be made to suffer as well. Only old Monsieur Julot was going to escape; she had seen Yves's eyes flick over him as if he was not worth the effort needed.

Marianne's fingers shook as she poured the coffee, first for Tante Monique and then for the notary, before pushing filled cups across to Yves and Bernard. She set the tray containing the cognac and glasses in front of Yves and went back to the cane armchair with her head in a whirl. What had she done? She had handed herself over to this cold, arrogant creature who had once been her friend, a man who obviously enjoyed making people suffer. Suddenly, nowhere on earth seemed as comforting as London; she should have stayed there, listened to Liz instead of haring off at the drop of a hat, putting her head in a noose. But it was done now.

Two hours later she faced him across the kitchen table. He had driven the others back down to the village, Tante and Bernard to the ugly, square house with the butcher's shop tacked on to its side and Monsieur Julot to the garage where Henri, the old mechanic, was waiting to drive him back to Rémy. Now Yves was back, his face inscrutable and his eyes coldly mocking her.

'Before we talk, we will eat,' she forestalled him, raising the cover of a casserole and sniffing the contents appreciatively. 'It smells quite good. I don't think I've forgotten all that I learned from Grand'mère. Will you fetch the wine?' She turned her back and busied herself with choosing plates, glasses and cutlery.

Yves crumbled a piece of bread between long brown fingers.

'Grand'mère wrote to you?' It was a flat statement that needed no answer, but she found herself nodding. 'She told you everything?'

'She told me the things which she thought were important.'

His next words surprised her.

'You are a little fool!' There was an unpleasant twist to his mouth. 'You come here with your ridiculous sentimentality. Pah! Do you think that you can play the good fairy, wave your wand of sweetness and light and all will be well?'

'I'm not being sentimental,' she objected gravely. 'I'm being practical. La Barrière was my home for more than ten years, I love it nearly as much as you do, it's the only real home I can remember. I would like it to be my home again.'

'And rather than let Tante and Bernard have it, you would be willing to marry me? Did you know that half the people in Serac blame me for Gisèle's death? Aren't you afraid that I might drive you out to *your* death?'

Marianne maintained an appearance of calm. 'Grand'mère told me that Gisèle was killed in a car crash on the hill. What were you supposed to have done? Engineered it? Fiddled with the brakes, perhaps?'

'I had reason enough.'

She shook her head at him. 'You have suggested that I live in a romantic dream, but you—you seem to live in a nightmare. It is you who have forgotten reality. This is your home as it once was mine, will you give it up so easily?' She watched the dark shadow flit across his face.

'You do not know me now, as I no longer know you.' The harsh voice assaulted her ears. 'We have both changed, we are no longer as we were. Look at you! Look at your hands, your clothes. How long is it since you scrubbed a floor, drew a chicken, fed hens? How long before you become bored and start longing for your city life and your smart friends?'

'I scrubbed this floor this morning. I also plucked and drew the chicken you are now eating, and I fed the hens before you came back and they are now safely shut up where the foxes can't reach them.' Marianne felt her temper slipping. 'As for becoming bored, there seems to be quite a lot to do in this house and we shall not have to live in each other's pockets.'

'And if that is not enough for me?' Yves's grey eyes held hers with a threat. 'Do you not fear for yourself, little English Miss? Remember, that I am said to have killed my wife when she wished to leave me.'

'Pooh!' Marianne wrinkled her nose in disgust. 'I find that very hard to believe.'

'You do not think I could kill?'

'I think you're trying to frighten me. Of course you could kill.' She kept it on a light note. 'You could beat a man to death with your fists or perhaps throttle him if you really lost your temper, but I don't think you could premeditate something. If you could have done that, you wouldn't have married Gisèle in the first place. You would have told her to go and father her bastard elsewhere.' She spoke confidently, although confidence was the last thing in her mind.

'I do not wish to hear such words from your lips,' he spoke coldly. 'They do not become my wife.'

Marianne felt herself go limp with relief.

Over coffee, Yves talked money, but she waved it aside. 'I have my own,' she protested, 'quite a lot. Grand'mère taught me to be frugal and I've always earned a good salary. Shall you object if I buy some new furniture?'

Yves's face, which had lost its chill momentarily, hardened again so that he scowled. 'You may choose what you want to buy, the bills will come to me.'

Marianne tried to inject a little humour into the proceedings. Now she had surmounted the first hurdle, the relief made her lighthearted.

'You'll regret that offer,' she told him with a smile. 'I would like new curtains throughout the house and there are a great many large windows in this house. It will cost you a packet! I've learned to like English curtains, they keep out the draughts.'

Yves reached for a pipe and tobacco from his pocket and made a little ritual of tapping the tobacco firmly into the bowl and lighting it. Through the blue haze of the smoke he watched her with narrowed eyes. Her grey-green eyes were quiet, almost grey now, and her wide mouth curved softly.

'Tomorrow,' he told her, 'we will go to Rémy. There is the matter of a betrothal ring—an outward symbol. There will have to be others.'

'Others?' She raised an enquiring glance. 'Oh! I see what you mean. We'll have to put on some sort of a show when there are people about.'

'Exactly. We can go into those details later—but for tomorrow, when you have chosen your ring, you may search for the materials for these curtains which you so much desire.' His eyes slid over her, taking in her light-weight suit and thin-soled, high-heeled shoes. 'You also need warmer clothing. Have you forgotten how cold the winter here can be?' His tone was disparaging and harsh.

'No,' she answered him comfortably, 'I haven't forgotten.' Her eyebrows raised as she took a sip of scalding coffee. 'Am I allowed to pay for my own clothes?'

'You may choose them,' he answered her flatteningly.

While Marianne washed up and tidied in the kitchen, Yves went off to his office to make a telephone call and returned just as she was putting away the last of the dishes. He shrugged himself into his sheepskin jacket and stood watching as she rinsed down the draining board.

'I am going to Madame Berthilot's,' he said shortly, and Marianne searched her memory and found a face to fit the name. Madame Berthilot was the village dressmaker, a small brown sparrow of a woman, forever twittering and fluttering. A widow with two children, a boy and a girl. Marianne remembered the boy as being several years younger than herself, but the girl she could not recall except as a chubby toddler in exquisitely embroidered dresses.

'Her daughter Sylvie wants work,' Yves frowned. 'I shall ask if she may come here. She is a good-tempered girl of no great intelligence or she would have left the village before now.' He sounded resigned, as though he deplored something but was powerless to prevent it.

Marianne was drying her hands on a kitchen towel. 'Let me come with you,' she suggested. 'I can speak to Madame Berthilot perhaps more easily than you.'

Yves nodded briefly, once again cold and remote, and Marianne decided that he had become silent through habit. He probably hardly spoke to anyone for weeks at a time, she reasoned, just made noises at the animals and threw a few orders around on the farm and down in the vineyard.

Madame Berthilot twittered and fluttered about, clearing a chair of a half-made dress and fetching wine and glasses. She remembered Marianne very well. 'All arms and legs, but the elegance was there, even when you were only a child.' Her eyes ran swiftly over Marianne's slender length, admiring the heavy swathe of marmalade-coloured hair brushed into a smooth chignon. 'And you are to be married, is it that you require a wedding dress?'

Marianne blinked with surprise. It was less than an hour ago that she had been sure of the marriage herself, until then it had been pure speculation on her part, yet already Serac Ste. Marie knew about it! She grimaced over Madame Berthilot's head at Yves, who smiled back sardonically.

'A better service than in the African jungle,' he spoke in English. 'Tante Monique can do it without drums!'

Marianne smiled down at a puzzled Madame Berthilot. 'Not a wedding dress, *madame*. It would not be proper so soon after Grand'mère's death. I shall wear ordinary day clothes.' Madame Berthilot twittered and Marianne soothed her. 'But I am in need of someone to help me in the house,' she made a moue of distress. 'Everything has been greatly neglected since Grand'mère became ill and there is a lot to do before the wedding. Monsieur Bersac tells me that your daughter Sylvie wants work, will you allow her to come to me?'

Perhaps it was the smile or the elegance or just that Madame Berthilot was one of those who did not believe Yves to be a murderer, Marianne did not know, but half an hour later when they left the little house, they were accompanied by an excited Sylvie, who plumped herself down in the back seat of the car together with a string bag containing what she would need for the next few days. She would live in until the wedding; it had been agreed then she would come daily.

As Yves had said, Sylvie was a good-tempered girl although a bit of a chatterbox. It would be good for Yves, decided Marianne. With Sylvie about the house, he would have to curb his ill humour and turn a less sardonic face to the world.

Back at La Barrière, after Sylvie had been tucked up in the small bedroom where Marianne herself had slept as a child; and after Yves had gone down to the *curé*'s house where he was staying for the next few weeks until the wedding, Marianne lay quietly in the bed in Yves's room and watched a pale sliver of moon swing in a shallow arc across the window while she put her thoughts in order.

Was she doing the right thing? She didn't know! She was doing what she had to do. She had seized an opportunity, and what would come of it was unforeseeable. She had loved Yves for eight long years and none of her friends had ever guessed, so why should he? It was going to be an icy relationship, but she thought she could bear that. He had become hard, bitter and suspicious and she would have to work hard to make him trust her.

There would have been other women, of course, but she

shrugged them off. Yves was a man, not a monk. It wasn't going to be any trip to Paradise, but it would have to be enough. It was all she could expect.

CHAPTER TWO

In the jeweller's shop in Rémy, Marianne seethed with indignation while Yves waved away the solitaires and the sapphires. This was supposed to be her choosing a betrothal ring and so far she had not even been consulted! Her attention wandered off to a shelf full of chased silver trifles and Yves had to grasp her arm to bring her straying attention back to the matter in hand.

He had settled on an emerald, a big, square-cut one mounted on a heavy gold hand and outlined in small diamonds. It looked ruinously expensive, and Marianne grimaced to herself as the jeweller moved the ring forward and discreetly put back several others which he had been displaying.

This ring did not have to be held up to the light and have its facets commented upon. It needed no attention drawn to its brilliance or the superb quality of its setting. It sat there in its little leather and velvet box and gleamed balefully at them, the green glow at its heart having an almost hypnotic effect. Marianne winced.

'I would prefer something less expensive, something more friendly. That looks as though it hates me!'

'It matches your eyes.' Yves had made up his mind. 'More green than grey.' He looked at the emerald again and reached for his wallet. 'On our anniversaries there will be other emeralds and soon you will have a collection.'

'I don't want a collection!' Marianne hissed so that the

jeweller would not hear her. 'If you want to spend that amount of money, why don't you buy yourself a new tractor or a piece of land, something of practical value, something that would show a profit?'

'Marianne, you have no romance in your soul!' His words robbed her of speech so that she could only gape at him while he pushed the ring on her finger. 'This has practical value, Marianne.' He moved the ring about, letting the sunlight light up the green flame at its heart. 'The value will not depreciate with inflation. In ten years' time it will buy two tractors.'

This was going too far! 'I'm very careless about jewellery,' she made a face at him. 'I shall be taking it off and putting it on all the time, heaven knows where it will get to. I'll probably lose it.'

'It is a good fit, not loose.' He turned the ring on her finger and looked at it with satisfaction. 'If you wear it all the time, you will not lose it.'

Marianne felt the ring cold and heavy on her finger and looked down at its magnificence. 'I can see myself making pastry with this on my hand, or feeding the hens,' she remarked tartly. Was this how it was going to be? she asked herself. Like the ring, a cold relationship that would weigh heavily upon her? She shivered and made a final plea. 'I'll have to take it off lots of times, it's sure to get lost.'

The subject seemed to bore him. 'If you lose it, I will buy you another.' A fugitive sunbeam that had strayed into the shop's dark interior caught the emerald as Marianne turned her hand and green fire blazed out like a cold flame trapped in the crystal. 'I'll never have a moment's peace of mind,' she muttered, while Yves ignored her and counted out a small fortune in francs.

Marianne spent the rest of the morning shopping happily for curtains. Yves had gone to the bank and then had some business to attend to and she was to meet him for lunch at one o'clock. This gave her a little more than two hours to comb Rémy for suitable curtaining, and she made the best of those two hours. In her bag was a list of priorities and right at the top came curtains for the salon. There was a ghost at La Barrière and it was up to her to exorcise it. The plump, white ghost of Gisèle.

In Marianne's mind, it inhabited the salon, and the only way she would ever get rid of it was to do the room over so that it looked completely different. Only after she had done that would she be able to tackle the dining room and then the bedrooms.

It was a sensible programme, she consoled herself. They would need somewhere comfortable to sit, they could not spend all their time in the kitchen, therefore she would need the services of a decorator, material for curtains and comfortable chairs. The curtains first, she decided, and then the chairs. After lunch, Yves should take her to the decorators where they could choose wallpaper and paint to fit in with her furnishings.

The curtains were easy. The windows at La Barrière were ill-fitting and let in a lot of draughts. The old-fashioned outside shutters with which the house was fitted had, over the years, rusted back on their hinges, since they were far too awkward to fasten, so Marianne chose a thick, heavy velvet in a pleasing shade of gold, as little like the present curtains as possible.

The material was expensive, but she justified the expense by deciding to make up the curtains herself. She had examined Grand'mère's old treadle sewing machine and found it still in good working order. A few evenings' work and she would have her curtains for the cost of the material.

The gold velvet made a bulky parcel, so she left it in the shop and went prowling for a couple of chairs and a couch to take the place of the green plush-covered, uncomfortable-looking furnishings of which Grand'mère had been so proud.

At the back of Rémy's one and only furniture shop, she found part of what she was looking for—two small Victorian armchairs, in deeply buttoned yellow velvet, standing on squat, bandy little legs. The proprietor pointed out sadly that these chairs were not new. He had bought them from a friend and had re-upholstered them himself. Marianne compared the upholstery with the swatch of curtaining in her bag and found the match near perfect.

'I would require a couch of about the same period.' She sketched with her hands the approximate size and followed the proprietor into his workroom at the back of the shop.

'It is not finished yet,' he said sadly as he pointed to a sofa with a low padded back and one rolled arm, half of which was still covered in dingy green striped satin.

Marianne paused fractionally, then caught sight of the ring on her finger. She had been given no choice over that! She would please herself about these pieces of furniture. If Yves didn't like them, he could sit in the kitchen!

Over lunch, she discussed it with Yves.

'It's just what I want,' she told him belligerently. 'I've bought them!'

There was a ghost of a smile on Yves's face as he poured wine for her. 'The furnishing of your house is your own business, Marianne,' he murmured mildly, and Marianne, who had been expecting at least one small argument, was taken aback.

After lunch, when the parcel of curtaining was safely bestowed in the Citroën's boot, they went back to the furniture shop where Yves inspected her purchase in a very thorough manner and after having tried out the chairs, pronounced himself satisfied. They walked to the decorator's and chose a plain cream paper for the walls, and Marianne began to feel a little better. The salon was going to look quite charming!

Outside the decorator's shop, Yves took her arm firmly

and led her along the narrow street to another shop, a deceptively simple shop whose window contained nothing but a carelessly tossed piece of black velvet upon which lay a large white silk rose.

Inside the shop, nothing was carelessly tossed and Madame Jeanne, the proprietress, pursed her lips and listened carefully.

Clothes for a wedding? A quiet wedding—there had been a bereavement? Madame Jeanne's sharp black eyes considered and measured. There was the very thing, if it was to Mademoiselle's taste. A model, not suitable for everyone but very chic. In the dressing room, she produced a dress in fine cream wool and Marianne found herself whisked into it. It would need the little adjustments, Madame Jeanne's words became muffled as she inserted pins. But as Mademoiselle could see, Marianne was turned as if she was a doll to face a full-length mirror, both fabric and cut were of an excellence rarely found outside Paris. Did not Monsieur agree?

Madame Jeanne dived back into her storeroom and returned triumphant with a loose coat in fine navy wool which she placed over the cream dress, suggesting that a wide-brimmed hat in plain navy would look charming on Mademoiselle's hair with perhaps a cream silk rose as decoration. Marianne found herself agreeing to navy shoes and silk gloves with perhaps a cream leather handbag.

'All these things can be found.' Madame Jeanne tapped the side of her nose and turned her attention to Yves, who was playing the part of an interested spectator.

It was a charming, elegant and subdued ensemble, was it not? And their grief at the recent loss of a loved one would be evident to all who attended the ceremony.

'Most suitable!' Yves reached for his cheque book, but Madame Jeanne waved it away while she stuck a few more pins in.

'It's going to cost the earth,' Marianne told him in English.

'So!' His eyes slid over her. 'Do you think that I begrudge you a wedding dress?'

A fugitive gleam in his eyes brought hot colour to her cheeks, and she made a great to-do of ensuring that the hem length was exactly to her liking.

The wedding was arranged for three weeks later, and those three weeks passed all too swiftly. Marianne and Sylvie, arrayed in voluminous white overalls, re-whitened the kitchen walls and stripped peeling paper from the walls in the salon. Two men and a boy came out from Rèmy to hang the new paper and paint the woodwork of the salon, and before the chairs and sofa could be delivered the two girls dragged the dull green carpet out on to the yard at the back of the house. The carpet smelled of damp and disuse.

Yves, passing, looked at it briefly, but for the two perspiring females he did not spare a glance. 'Burn it!' he advised. Marianne took no notice, either of him or of what he said. As if he was not there, she spoke to Sylvie.

'It's a good carpet, old but good and very little worn. We'll beat it and clean it. There's no point in destroying it, for the colour is excellent and it will last many more years.'

So the carpet was beaten, sponged and then hung over a low wall to air in the still warm autumn sun.

'Burn that too.' Yves pointed at the sagging cane chair by the kitchen fire. It was evening and he had come in for dinner. It was the only time that Marianne held any conversation with him during the day. He would wash at the kitchen sink, stripped to the waist as if to emphasise his peasant status, then he would sit and eat whatever she had cooked, usually in a morose silence. Afterwards he would disappear into the room which was his office and later a curt 'Goodnight' would be flung at her before he reached for his jacket and went off to the *curé*'s house. Marianne shrugged. He was making her cross!

'There is a bathroom in this house,' she ignored the cold impersonality of the face he turned on her, 'Or there is a pump in the yard. You will *not* wash yourself in my kitchen. If you don't wish to use the bathroom, you can strip and I'll pump water for you and over you as Grand'mère did when you were young.'

'She did it to you once when you fell in the duckpond and came home covered in slime.' Yves sounded warmer and softer, as if he was back in the old days. 'You stank,' he reminded her. Marianne ignored what seemed to be a pointless piece of nostalgia.

'Which is it to be?' she demanded. 'Bathroom or pump?'

'Bathroom, if you insist, *mademoiselle*. Pardon me, but I forget you are nearly mistress here. The smell of sweat offends you?'

Marianne looked at her hands, no longer white and soft, nor were the nails perfect and polished to a soft pink. Grimly she choked back the words that threatened to spill from her tongue.

'I have no objection to the smell of sweat. I've sweated quite a bit myself these last two weeks.' She looked round at the fresh paint in the kitchen, at the gleaming floor tiles and the shining pans on the dresser. None of it was his work. Yet he could have helped had he wished. He could have helped lug out that carpet instead of leaving her and Sylvie to sweat over it.

He was being deliberately unco-operative, she decided, trying to make her lose her temper or make her so fed up that she would give up and go back to England. Well, it wouldn't work! As she carried the casserole across to the table, she asked.

'What's wrong with the bathroom?'

'Too full of feminine fripperies for a plain farmer.' Yves wrinkled his nose in a grimace of distaste. 'Bottles of bath oils and essences. Foamy stuff. Tins of talcum.'

She raised her eyebrows at him. So he'd been investigating! 'There's no need for you to use them.' She kept her voice steady, it would never do to let him think that she was laughing at him. 'I'll provide you with a cake of carbolic soap and you can come to dinner smelling of that!'

'Mademoiselle is too kind!' and he went off to the cellar to fetch a bottle of wine.

'Red!' she called after his retreating back. 'We're having beef.'

She opened the oven door, listening to the soft spluttering of the meat and sniffing the mouthwatering odour. The young carrots glistened redly in the dish beneath their glaze of melted butter and the haricots verts were a good strong green. Why did she bother? It would serve him right if she slapped down a tin of meat on the table together with a loaf of bread, if she bought soup in tins and opened one for him! He didn't deserve. . . . Yes, he did! She thought about Gisèle and her mouth twisted bitterly. She had known all about Gisèle, even before she left school, she had known about Gisèle and Yves had married her! Quiet, fastidious Yves! Not too fastidious, though, he had admitted that.

Thinking along those lines would only make her angry, and that wouldn't serve her purpose. She had to be calm, reasonable and practical for quite some time yet.

Later that evening she raised her head from the yellow velvet seam she was stitching and took her foot from the treadle so that the machine slowed to a clanking halt. Now what? She surveyed her unexpected and, as far as she was concerned, unwelcome guests over the top of the sewing machine, and set her face in the expression which had taken her so long to achieve when she had started in the business world. A cool, quiet, slightly smiling expression, while inwardly she raged.

'Do come in.' She allowed a tinge of sarcasm to colour the words. Tante Monique and Bernard were already in!

Tante had pushed open the kitchen door and entered without even a tap and Bernard had followed his mother like Mary's little lamb. If they had expected to catch her and Yves *in flagrante delicto*, or whatever the Latin tag was, they were doomed to disappointment. Marianne smiled inwardly at the ridiculous thought. Yves make love in a kitchen! He had a better sense of occasion than that!

Tante Monique's eyes ranged around the room, tidy and immaculate except for the clutter of gold velvet on the big table. She peered into each corner as if suspecting Yves to have concealed himself somewhere.

'Where is Monsieur Bersac?' Her flat, harsh voice made an accusation of the question.

'Not here, as you see,' Marianne permitted herself a faint shrug. 'He might be in the room where he does his accounts—if not, I have no idea where you might find him.'

Tante came and fingered the velvet, her sharp, boot-button eyes assessing the quality and calculating the price per metre. 'You have expensive tastes, *mademoiselle*.'

Marianne nodded tranquilly. 'It is possible, *madame*, but Yves is reasonably wealthy. He chose this material, it will look very well, do you not think so?' She was bending the truth a bit, she knew. Yves had merely complimented her on her choice, but Tante wasn't to know that.

Bernard chose this moment to interrupt his mother. His eyes, pebbly in his round, plump face, were watching Tante with something very like fright on their flat, wet surfaces. There was no depth to Bernard's eyes.

'We were worried for your safety, Marianne. Here, alone in this farmhouse which is so remote from the village.'

'My safety?' Marianne let a little surprise creep into her face. 'Who would hurt me? I am sure that at La Barrière I am as safe as I would be in the middle of London.' Her lips twisted very slightly. London was not all that safe!

'Accidents happen, Marianne.' Bernard was lugubrious and his mother nodded significantly.

Marianne reached for the scissors and trimmed a length of cotton from the curtain she was stitching. 'Accidents?' She looked Bernard full in his nasty little eyes. 'You are perhaps referring to the rumours concerning Yves and Gisèle? I do not believe them.'

'Gisèle was a sweet girl.' Tante's face was unbecomingly flushed and her tight mouth, outlined in a raspberry-coloured lipstick which went ill with her high-coloured complexion, tightened further.

Marianne raised a polite eyebrow and gave the older woman a look of patent disbelief. 'I knew Gisèle.' She spoke quietly and her voice, kept deliberately unemotional, spoke volumes.

At that moment, the door opened and Yves came in from his office. At the sight of his aunt and cousin his face became even more forbidding.

'Tante Monique and Bernard came to assure themselves of my safety.' Unconcernedly, Marianne pinned ruffling tape to the curtain.

'You are in danger?' Yves was sarcastic and Marianne shrugged.

'I don't think so.'

'Their concern is . . . interesting.' He hesitated slightly before the last word and turned to reach for his jacket, slinging it carelessly about his shoulders. 'How long before Sylvie returns?'

'About an hour, I think.' She glanced at her watch. 'Perhaps two, although Jacques promised me that they wouldn't be late. There's a dance in Rèmy, I don't know what time it finishes.'

Yves, expressionless, turned back to his aunt and her son.

'You walked? I will drive you back.'

Tante made a little ceremony of her adieus and Bernard

clasped Marianne's hand, giving it a little squeeze. Left alone, Marianne went to the sink and washed her hands thoroughly to remove the feel of Bernard, then she sat at the table, her chin in her hands. The yellow velvet curtains had lost their appeal and she had lost the enthusiasm for sewing them. Thoughts crowded into her head and for the first time since she had knelt beside Grand'mère's bed, she felt doubt. Not about Yves and the old scandal, she was almost sure that it was just malicious gossip, but was she doing the right thing? This would be the second time that Yves would marry at his grandmother's bidding. It was the second time that the old lady would have forced him to choose between what he wanted and La Barrière. It would be the second time that she had forced an unwelcome wife on him. She frowned and then her face cleared.

What utter nonsense! Grand'mère's will could have been set aside. Any clever lawyer could have pleaded that the terms were unreasonable and any judge would have agreed with that plea. If she knew this, then so did Yves. He had no need to marry her at all, not even to keep La Barrière. Therefore he was either marrying her to please a dead woman or to please himself. She hoped it was to please himself.

Abruptly, she rose and cleared away the clutter of sewing. Tomorrow she would finish the curtains and hang them, then she would phone down to Rémy and have her chairs and sofa delivered—and while she was about it, she decided defiantly, she would give the plumber a ring.

Upstairs, across the corridor from Yves's room there was a small room, barely more than a large cupboard. If the water pipes and the drains were in the right places, she would have it turned into a shower room for Yves, a spartan place with plain white tiles, and when it was finished, she would toss in a cake of plain soap and a few rough white towels. Let him complain about that!

Yves did not complain. He merely raised his eyebrows

at the plumber's presence, which fortunately did not last above two days, and said nothing until after the shower was finished. Marianne took in the thick, rough towels and the cake of carbolic soap. It was spartan enough for the most dedicated athlete, she thought grimly, or for a misogynist!

'I have paid the plumber.' Yves sounded faintly amused.

'I didn't want your masculine, misogynistic person to be further offended by my feminine fripperies.' Marianne had been practising this little speech and was rather pleased with it. 'Does it suit you?'

'Better than the bathroom, which is beginning to smell like a harem.' He went on eating her good onion soup. 'Why can women never be satisfied? They have a warm, feminine smell of their own. Why drown it in lotions?'

'How like a man!' Marianne raised her eyes to heaven. 'You would soon complain if I went around smelling of that warm, feminine smell of which you sound so fond. You'd start bringing me little gifts of bath salts and scented soap.'

This bit of mild repartee was as much as she would allow herself at the moment. It would have been so easy to have lost her temper with him, to have yelled and screamed, but that was what Gisèle had done. Later, she promised herself, when she was more sure of her ground.

The day after tomorrow was her wedding day and deliberately she withdrew into silence, checking the house over in her mind. Everything was ready, and the salon was a great success.

The dull moss green of the carpet set the chairs, sofa and curtains glowing. In one of the upstairs room she had found a small marquetry table. The top lifted to disclose a workbox with a red satin lining and small compartments to hold reels of thread and scissors, needles and a thimble. She had carried it down and set it beside her chair in the salon. This, together with the chairs, sofa and a glass-fronted cabinet which contained bottles and glasses was all the furniture that the room contained. It was enough, she thought.

Upstairs, she and Sylvie had cleaned the bedrooms thoroughly. Sylvie had moved into another small, cell-like room, and Marianne had returned to the room which she had occupied as a child. Grand'mère's bedroom had been cleared of bedding, cleaned and closed. That room was for the master and mistress of the house. Somehow she did not think that she and Yves would be on those sort of terms. Not yet, anyway.

On the day before her wedding, she drove down into Rémy marvelling at how long the autumn was lasting. There were roses still blooming in some of the gardens and the skies were a clear, untroubled blue. These were the golden days, possibly the last before winter. Marianne shivered at the possible omen.

Yves had refused to accompany her. He had faced her across the table, his face a mask of indifference.

'Are you not capable of driving yourself?'

Marianne had nodded serenely and occupied herself with checking the contents of her bag so that her disappointment would not show. The way he had spoken made the words sound like an insult and the sarcasm had set her teeth on edge. Worse was to come. He had tossed a roll of notes down on to the table top.

'Buy yourself a wedding present,' he had growled.

'A present is a present,' she had told him gravely. 'It's a gift. I can't buy my own wedding present.'

'Then do without.' His shrug had been eloquent of uninterest. 'Buy anything you like.'

By eye she had assessed the thickness of the wad of money and its possible value. About five hundred pounds sterling, she judged, and she had taken great pleasure in walking away and leaving it lying there, not sparing it or him a backward glance.

In Rémy, Madame Jeanne had been as good as her word. The coat, dress and shoes were ready and the hat and gloves lay beside them. The shoes were an unnecessary extravagance, since Marianne already had a pair of navy shoes which she intended to wear. They were to be the 'something old' part of her wedding outfit. These new ones she would put away, she'd decided after examining them with admiration. Italian made, light as a feather, they would make her feet look incredibly slender; she would save them for special occasions.

Madame Jeanne also produced some fragile underwear together with a gorgeous nightgown in apple green silk, lavishly trimmed with lace and, beside it, a frothy nonsense of a négligé. None of these things were of her ordering and Marianne raised her eyebrows at the proprietress.

Madame Jeanne smirked. 'Monsieur Yves,' she murmured, a look as old as Eve on her dark, sharp face. 'He chose the green, although I told him that it was not considered a fortunate colour for a bride. He said,' again she smirked, 'that it was the only colour for you!'

Marianne produced her travellers' cheques, but these were waved aside. Monsieur had already paid!

She stopped the Mini in the farmyard of La Barrière and carefully carried her beautifully wrapped parcels, with the hat box balanced on the top, into the kitchen. As she set them down on the table, she stopped aghast and stared at the gleaming white gas cooker which stood in one corner of the room. Alongside of the dresser stood an equally white and gleaming refrigerator. There was nobody about and with a puzzled frown she went into the pantry. Everything was as usual except that under the lowest shelf stood a row of gas cylinders, one of which was connected to a copper pipe that vanished through the wall into the kitchen. A wedding present after all! She went back to the kitchen and looked at the old range. It was lit, but the fire was low. With care, she added logs. She would cook on the range tonight; she would not use the new cooker until tomorrow, her wedding day.

When Yves came in for his meal he scowled to see her shifting a meat dish from the old oven and hastily she spoke.

'I'm not used to gas. I shall need a demonstration, I didn't want to blow myself up.' With relief, Marianne saw his scowl lessening and was glad of the heat from the range to mask the flush which had risen to her cheeks.

'The generator is not powerful enough to cope with an electric cooker.' He fiddled with the taps. 'It manages the lights and the immersion heater for hot water, but a cooker would overload it. I'll show you how to use this one after dinner, there's nothing complicated about it. Did you finish your shopping?'

Marianne nodded and smiled. 'Everything, down to the last pin. There was a lot of stuff I didn't order, though, expensive stuff.'

'You probably have better of your own,' he said flatly. 'Madame Jeanne seemed to think you should be new from top to toe, so I told her to see to it.' Marianne turned away to hide a smile. Yves was not going to admit to one second of weakness!

'No, nothing better, nothing even like! I told you, I'm frugal. Strictly utilitarian underneath, that's me.' Marianne heard herself prattling on and tried very hard to stop, since Yves was looking as though he was not interested.

When he had demonstrated the gas cooker, she asked idly, 'Why did you never get this sort of thing for Grand'mère? It would have saved her a lot of work.'

The smile he turned on her was not pleasant. 'Grand'mère looked on hard work as a sort of penance, didn't you know? Anything which would have stopped her doing her penance was an invention of the devil. I don't know what sins she thought she had committed, possibly the fact that while she loved children, she thought any form of sex was sinful.' He slanted a wry smile down at Marianne. 'And yet the old lady must have indulged in it at least once before my father was born. Perhaps she felt relief when my grandfather died. Grand'mère used work as a sort of self-castigation, and anything which would diminish that work was not to be thought of.'

Marianne tried to hide the horror on her face. 'What a beastly thing to say!' and then she stopped quickly, regretting her outburst. This was the first time since she had returned to La Barrière that Yves had spoken more than one sentence to her, the first time he had spoken what was in his mind. 'I don't remember her like that,' she murmured.

'No, you wouldn't,' he jeered. 'Good little Marianne was a girl, wasn't she? Not one of the sinful male sex.'

The next morning, Sylvie helped her dress and Marianne studied the weather from the bedroom window. It was a sunny day for the end of October. Happy the bride the sun shines on! She inspected her face in the small mirror. Brides were supposed to be radiant, weren't they? Have an inner glow? She couldn't see any trace of radiance on her face nor any inner glow. She pulled the navy hat well down and hid behind the wide brim.

At ten o'clock precisely, a hired car bumped into the yard to take her down to the church where Yves was waiting for her. He looked a complete stranger, and for a second her courage deserted her and she wanted to turn tail and run, but the small church was full, crowded with the inhabitants of Serac Ste. Marie, and Sylvie was pressing a tight posy of late cream rosebuds into her cold hands.

The service was brief, and when it was over Marianne got into Yves's old Citroën for the long drive to Rémy, where they went through the civil ceremony in the Hotel de Ville and Sylvie and her boy-friend gleefully gave everybody sugared almonds in little white satin bags.

Now she and Yves were quite alone. Sylvie would no longer be staying the nights and the farmhouse was strangely silent. Marianne prepared dinner on her new gas cooker, although the fire was lit in the range. After dinner, Yves retired to his office. He said 'Goodnight' before he went and closed the door of the room behind him with a firm thud of finality, leaving Marianne to wash up and tidy everything away before she went to her own room.

Slowly and with a cold heart, she undressed, feeling extraordinarily tired. The gorgeous nightie and the unsuitable négligé she left in their box and hid them away at the bottom of the wardrobe. It wasn't going to be that sort of a wedding night.

In her narrow bed, she lay awake for a while taking stock. She thought that she had done very well and it would be a pity to spoil it now. It was well after midnight when she heard Yves come up the stairs. He stumbled on the top step and Marianne, snuggling down, drew the pillow further under her cheek.

She would not think of the future; from where she was standing it looked very dreary and grim. She would take each day as it came, expecting nothing, then she could not be disappointed.

CHAPTER THREE

MARIANNE had meant to be up early on this, the first morning of her married life, but she slept through the small, refined ring of her travel alarm clock. She had set it for six, but it was nearly nine when she woke. For a moment she could not think what she was doing here, and then the mists of sleep cleared away and she remembered. She was no longer Miss Mary Anne Montgomery, she was now Madame Bersac and apparently failing in her duties.

Hastily she thrust her feet into slippers, bundled on her dressing gown and patterned along the corridor to the top of the stairs. This took her past Yves's bedroom; the door was open and the room was empty. She gave a hurried glance around, noting the unmade bed and then went to listen carefully in the corridor. There was no noise from downstairs, which meant that Yves had left the house. Holding up the long skirts of her dressing gown, Marianne went quietly down the stairs and into the kitchen. The fire was made and the room warm; the coffee pot was warm too and she pushed it over to boil while she collected herself a cup and saucer.

Sitting at the table, she planned her day. Yves would be in at lunchtime, perhaps. She would make some soup, just in case he came, and for dinner tonight there were escalopes of veal with mushrooms. Her eyes fell on the new cooker. A wedding present? He could keep it! She would use the old range just as Grand'mère had done. This late in the year, it was not warm enough to do without a fire, and if the range was hot, why waste gas?

But between now and lunchtime and lunchtime and dinner, she had to occupy herself somehow. She would start on the dining room.

Accordingly, her soup prepared and simmering nicely, she went off to the dining room arrayed in a pair of old jeans and a dark green sweater. Her hair was tied back with a piece of narrow ribbon and she had slipped her feet into a pair of comfortable sandals. Her mind ran ahead.

This afternoon she would write to young Mr Gillespie, the big, middle-aged man who was the son of old Mr Gillespie who had wanted to put her in a school. She would ask him to come over himself or send someone to help her. He would give her advice on making a will and perhaps send one of his clerks around to help Liz with the packing of her personal belongings, arrange the sale of various articles which she would no longer require and see to the shipment of the rest to La Barrière.

She would also write to Liz and bring her up to date. Perhaps Liz would call on the way to Switzerland; she hoped so.

Meanwhile, there was the dining room. What was needed was a survey to determine what had to be done to make the room habitable. Marianne opened the door and looked around grimly.

It was nearly as bad as the salon had been, nearly but not quite. Here the floor was of polished parquet, so there was no great carpet to drag about. If the paper was stripped from the walls and several coats of cream paint applied, the room would look much brighter. She tried to see it in her mind's eye. The table and chairs needed re-polishing and the chair seats would have to be re-upholstered. Brown velvet curtains, she thought. She could do most of the work herself; it was obvious that she was going to have plenty of time.

A movement behind her sent her swinging around. It was much too early for Yves and people here observed a certain delicacy. Nobody would dream of visiting a newly married couple for at least three days, surely?

Bernard stood behind her in the doorway.

'I didn't hear you knock.' Irritation boiled up within her.

'But we are now cousins, are we not?' Bernard smiled deprecatingly. 'And between cousins, we do not need to be so formal, surely?'

'I think, if you don't mind, *cousin*,' she stressed the word, 'you had better call me Madame Bersac. It's a new name to me and I like the sound of it. I must get used to using it.' She surveyed him dispassionately. 'How did you get in, and what are you doing here anyway? You won't find Yves here at this time of day. He won't be home before lunch time at the earliest, he may not even come then.'

Bernard smiled, a lovely innocent smile that set Marianne's teeth on edge.

'I came to see you, to assure myself of your wellbeing and safety. As for how I entered the house, I came through the front door, it isn't locked.' Bernard managed to sound virtuous, smug and conspiratorial all at one and the same time, and Marianne glared at him, her temper teetering on a knife edge.

'What did you expect to find?' she demanded tartly. 'My dead body lying at the foot of the stairs? Don't be stupid, Bernard!' There was a nasty glitter in her eyes which had become a definite green. She went swiftly past him and into the kitchen were she flung open the door on to the yard.

'Thank you for your solicitude, but it's quite unnecessary and I find your presence here today in very bad taste. Now, please go,' she gestured towards the open door. 'If you want to come again, come in the evening when my husband is at home and knock, like any other visitor. Cousinship doesn't give you the right to walk into this house without so much as a by-your-leave. I don't like people wandering around my house uninvited, and I have far too much to do to be bothered with morning callers.'

'You do not understand, Marianne,' Bernard hesitated. 'When you were a girl, before you left to go to England, I....'

She did not let him finish. Her memories of Bernard's hands touching, patting her were quite vivid still.

'Stop that! I don't want to hear it. I remember you very well when I was a girl. I remember your hot little hands trying to paw me. I didn't like it then and I haven't changed a bit. Goodbye!' And with a feeling of profound satisfaction, she slammed the door in his face.

Maybe it *was* bad manners on her part, perhaps she should not have spoken so brusquely, but a rage was simmering within her. She marched through the hall to the little-used front door. As Bernard had said, it was unlocked and there was no sign of a key, but there were two substantial looking bolts. She shot these across and went into the office where she dialled the number of the hardware business in Rémy.

Just before lunchtime a man was busy changing the locks on both front and back doors at La Barrière. Yves, coming in to lunch, paused and watched the workman with surprise on his face. Marianne said nothing until they were both seated, eating soup. Then she explained.

'Bernard was here this morning. He came in through the front door without knocking. I turned around and there he was, right behind me; so I've had the locks changed on both doors and the front one is going to be bolted from now on.' She eyed her husband severely. 'Being your cousin doesn't mean that he can have the run of the house, not while I'm in it. I told him that he could come in the evenings when you're at home.' She paused for breath and then continued, 'Do you know what he told me? He told me that he wanted to assure himself of my safety!' She was indignant and the emotion brought a soft colour to her cheeks and her eyes glinted very green. 'By the way,' she tore a piece from a rather stale loaf, 'I'm going to write a couple of letters this afternoon and I shall drive down to post them. I'll try to get some fresh bread while I'm there. Is there anything that you want?'

'No!' The vehemence in his voice surprised her and she looked at him with startled eyes. 'Write your letters and if you prefer not to trust me to post them for you, I will take you down and you may post them yourself, but you do not drive that car of yours anywhere. Do you understand?'

'No, I don't understand. I drove the Mini to Rémy only the day before yesterday. . . .'

'I do not wish to lose another wife on that hill.'

'But as I said,' she argued, 'I drove the Mini only the

day before yesterday.'

'The day before yesterday you were not my wife, Marianne.' His eyes glittered disagreeably and Marianne subsided into silence.

The following day, Yves gave himself a holiday. Marianne found him in the kitchen when she came down at half past seven, and looked her surprise at him.

'A business meeting in Rémy this morning,' he explained briefly. 'I thought we could both go. You can look around the shops while I get this meeting over—you mentioned something about more curtains yesterday. We will meet for lunch and make a leisurely trip home. We could go to the cinema if you like.'

Carefully she schooled her face. Yves, the dedicated, in a cinema? The mind boggled! 'You're sure you can spare the time?' she asked sweetly. 'You don't need to alter your routine for me. As I said before, I have the Mini and I can drive myself anywhere I want to go.'

'And I have told you,' it was almost a snarl, '*you* will not drive anywhere.'

Quietly she poured herself another cup of coffee. 'If you say so,' she sighed almost pathetically. 'If I'm not allowed to drive myself anywhere, I might as well sell the car. We could put the money towards a more serviceable vehicle, a Land Rover perhaps. It would be useful in the bad weather. It's a shame to use your old Citroën—it's practically a vintage piece and I love that car,' she murmured idly, then almost thinking aloud, 'We wouldn't get much for the Mini here in France, not with it being a right-hand drive. It would be better to get it back to England and sell it there, small cars are booming now and it's in very good condition.'

'You go too fast, *madame*.' She watched as a small smile curved his mouth. 'I say that you are not to drive anywhere and you are already back in England, selling your Mini.'

'It was just a thought,' she said mildly. 'I didn't realise that I'd said it aloud, but I'm quite right about the Land Rover. They've a marvellous clearance and lots of gears. You can get them with a four-wheel drive and they're very practical in bad weather, especially on these hills and mountain roads. You need a practical vehicle here. You could use it to get from the farm to the vineyard, carry lambs and calves, all sorts of things,' she was warming to the theme. 'You could have a tow-bar fitted and tow things about.'

'As a saleswoman for Land Rovers, you are excellent.' Yves examined his empty coffee cup. 'As an interior decorator, you show promise. How are you at pouring coffee and feeding hens?'

Marianne flushed and poured his coffee. 'The bread isn't fresh, I'll toast it.' She reached for the toasting fork that hung by the oven and his hand closed over hers.

'See to your hens, Marianne,' he directed. 'I will attend to breakfast.'

It was a lovely day in Rémy, bright and cold, and Marianne, warmly wrapped in a sheepskin coat, was quite comfortable. Yves left her once the car was parked, he would meet her for lunch at one o'clock, so until then she had the somewhat restricted and limited resources of Rémy at her disposal. She shopped for curtaining and found a heavy velvet, just right for her purpose and in the bitter chocolate shade which she had wanted but didn't think she would obtain so easily. She also found some gold cord and tassels to relieve the rather sombre brown of the curtains and also some ready-frilled white muslin to go on the windows.

The little man in the furniture shop joyfully agreed to come with an assistant to polish the table top and he would take the chairs back with him to be polished and to have their tapestry seats renewed.

At the butcher's she dithered between steak and veal

and then remembered her new refrigerator and bought both, filling up a corner of her shopping bag with a sausage of noble proportions and a hundred-gramme pack of pâté. Then she betook herself to Madame Jeanne's in search of a long, warm dress to wear in the winter evenings. Madame Jeanne expressed regret, she had dresses but nothing that was suitable for Madame. 'Something could be found, of course, but there would be a small delay. Perhaps, if Madame could come in next week . . .?'

Lunch was also very pleasant. Yves had stopped snarling. He came into the restaurant, tall and bulky in his sheepskin jacket, and there was almost a smile on his face. Well, if not a smile, Marianne thought, a look of satisfaction.

'You've bought something,' she hazarded a guess. 'What is it, land, cattle or machinery?'

'Land.' He sat down opposite her and reached for the menu. 'What made you think that?'

'Your face—it looked satisfied, as if something you've been wanting for a long time has just dropped in your lap.'

'It is only a small corner of ground, but it rounds off the vineyard on the south side, and as you said, I have been waiting for it for a long time.' Hastily, he made his face expressionless. 'But I shall have to watch my expressions, you see too much. I forget that you have grown up. When you were younger, your eyes were very expressive and clear although they did not see so much. Now they see more, but your face is not so revealing. When did you learn to hide your feelings? In London?'

'No, here!' she wanted to scream at him. 'Here at La Barrière, when you married Gisèle.' But of course she couldn't say any such thing out loud, so she contented herself with what she hoped was a mysterious look.

'What do you think would happen to a commercial secretary if she let her feelings show?' She wrinkled her nose. 'Just imagine, it's five o'clock and the poor girl is tired and fed up, and then the boss comes in with half a dozen letters which he says have to catch the evening post. Do you know what happens? The poor girl pins a sweet smile on her face and says "Certainly, Mr So-and So" and goes back to work. Then, of course, she has to take the blame when the boss forgets his wife's birthday, forgets an important engagement and suddenly decides he doesn't want to see someone who's been waiting in the office for hours. After about three months of that sort of thing, you learn to conceal your feelings pretty well.'

The little cinema in Rémy was not showing anything worthwhile, an American film that had been dubbed in French, and Marianne always found dubbed films very confusing, the words and the lip movements so rarely coincided, so they decided to return to La Barrière after a leisurely lunch. It was growing dark now by five in the evening and travelling on winding, mountain roads in the half light was not Marianne's cup of tea. As soon as the bulky pack of curtaining was bestowed in the boot, she settled herself firmly in the car for the journey home. Almost at once, she sensed a change in Yves. He was silent and his face had become cold and enigmatic again.

Once in the house, she went upstairs to change into slacks and a jumper and was just hanging away her suit when she became aware of him standing in the doorway of her cell-like bedroom. She stood quietly in the fading light, the coat-hanger in one hand and the jacket of her suit in the other, her eyes questioning.

He came all the way into the room, closing the door behind him, his size making the narrow room seem even smaller.

'Sylvie comes back tomorrow morning,' he almost growled the words as he leant with his back against the door.

'So?' Marianne forced a noncommittal reply and waited for the rest of whatever it was he had to say. When it came, it surprised her.

'Eight years ago, I was known far and wide throughout the district as the man who did not sleep with his wife. I've no fancy for that again.'

'You want a proper marriage?' Her heart turned a complete somersault and then started beating again erratically.

'If you do not find it distasteful.' In the gloom she could just make out his face, expressionless and the heavy lids fallen, hooding his eyes. 'We could pretend, but. . . .'

'You don't think you could keep up the pretence, is that it?' She forced a slight smile to her lips, just in case he could see her face clearly, and she tried to inject a little humour into the words.

Yves shrugged. 'It would not be a pretence for long, I am not made of wood. I have all the normal appetites. A night would come and you would be there. . . .' his voice tailed off, leaving the rest to her imagination.

'And if I was not willing?' How long would he keep her standing here in the semi dark? she agonized silently. Then she felt his hand heavy on her shoulder as he took the coat-hanger and jacket from her unresisting fingers and tossed them on the bed. He turned her slowly to face him, as if he was savouring every separate second, his hands warm on the bare skin of her shoulders. With the same slow deliberation he pulled her against him, sliding his hands down her back, moulding her body to his own. She seemed to be incapable of any movement of her own, she could only watch as his face came down to meet hers. She noticed that his eyes were closed and then there was the seeking demand of his mouth on hers, the slow caress of his hands through the thin silk of her slip, and Marianne ceased to think and only felt.

When at last Yves raised his head and opened his eyes, the grey slits were no longer cold and his voice had changed. The hard impersonal tone had vanished, to be replaced by one of dry amusement.

'You might find it to your taste, *madame*.'

'Gisèle didn't find it to her taste.' Remorselessly Marianne prodded a sore spot, hurting herself while she tried to gather up her scattered wits and restore herself to some semblance of calm.

'Gisèle was not to my taste!' He captured her hand and held it. 'Once and once only, when I was drunk. Never again!'

'And since?' She moved cold fingers in his.

'Rèmy, Clermont, Paris. Not often. Someone I did not know, who did not know me. Never in the village.'

Marianne wrinkled her nose at him distastefully. 'That would have to stop!'

'Of course, *madame*.' He was dry, matter-of-fact. 'When a man can eat at home, he does not need to look for restaurants.'

So that was how she was to be regarded—something on a plate at home, a tray in bed! Temper flared hotly, but she thrust it down. Yves's original reason cut both ways. Marianne did not fancy the sniggers of the village either. Bernard would soon hear of it and so would Tante Monique! A wife who was not a wife—Tante would spread that juicy bit of gossip as far as she could stretch it. And Yves had been honest, he hadn't tried to pretend that he loved her. He had let her know what he wanted and shown her what he could give in return, and he'd done it without saying a word. She was grateful for that, in a way. She heard herself say, with a calm that astounded her.

'I'll move my things into your room after supper. The feminine fripperies will not upset you?'

'I expect I shall be able to accept them with equanimity, perhaps even grow used to them.' He paused, looking through the window into the gathering darkness. 'I will help you to move your belongings and tomorrow morning we will not rise early. That way, Sylvie will have no spectacular news to take back to the village.'

If this conversation continued on these lines, Marianne thought, she would be sick. It was cold, remote, horrid! Abruptly she changed the subject.

'Sylvie is going to bring fresh bread with her each morning and croissants, if they're ready. I'm looking forward to my breakfast tomorrow morning.' With hardly any effort at all she turned a quiet smile upon him.

After supper she carried her clothes into Yves's bedroom, hanging them in the huge black oak wardrobe. Another trip cleared her dressing table and Yves came with a bundle of shoes. In a finicky fashion, Marianne arranged them in a neat row at the bottom of the wardrobe before going back to her own narrow room.

'There's not much more,' he was waiting for her. 'I'm having the rest of my clothes sent over. That was what my letter was about, the one you posted for me. Mr Gillespie will see to it all. There isn't a lot to come and there's loads of room in that wardrobe. I doubt if you'll even notice the difference. No,' she went past him towards the bed, intent on stripping it, 'leave the suitcases where they are, I'll have Sylvie take them up to one of the attics tomorrow.' Competently, she began on the bed, pulling off pillowcases.

'And this?' Yves held up the box containing the nightgown and négligé which he had fished out from the bottom of the wardrobe.

'I didn't think it was quite me.' She turned back to the bed and made herself busy folding sheets into a neat pile, topping them with the pillowcases; the blankets were already lying on a chair by the bed. Taking the white bedspread, she flung it over the bare mattress before she turned back to him. 'I'm the tailored type,' she nodded at the box in his hand, 'even in bed. Garments of that style and quality are completely wasted on me.' She managed a cool, composed expression, she even smiled, although how she did it, she didn't know. 'That's the lot.' The steadiness of her voice surprised her. 'Shall we go downstairs for a while? I put fresh coffee on the stove, it should be ready by now, and you can have cognac with yours.'

When she went upstairs the nightgown lay in pale green silken folds across the bottom of his bed. A bit more window-dressing for Sylvie! Angrily, she replaced her pyjamas in the drawer of the enormous chest, and with regret too. They were much warmer than this silk and lace confection. Scowling, she gathered up the green silk and headed for the bathroom where she ran a deep, hot bath and dowsed the surface liberally with a pungently scented bath essence. Lying in the bath, she tried to talk sense to herself. This was what she had wanted, wasn't it? This was what she had waited eight years for, so why had several large butterflies taken up residence in her stomach?

Outwardly calm, she dried herself and let the nightgown slip over her head and down, before she made her way back to the bedroom, where she posed before the long mirror in the door of the old-fashioned wardrobe. She had never worn anything quite as glamorous or luxurious as this before—nor so becoming either, she admitted grudgingly.

'You look very romantic,' she told her reflection, then put out her tongue at it. Romantic! This face-saving operation! An operation arranged in a businesslike impersonal way. No romance there! She shivered as a cold draught curled around her ankles and she climbed swiftly into bed. *His* bed. Which side should she take? Deliberately she kept her mind on mundane things, little things, trifles which would stop her thinking about what she was doing, because if she thought about that then she *would* be sick, and she couldn't think of anything less romantic than a bilious bride. What did it matter which side of the bed she slept on? Let Yves take the other one, she decided morosely, and then the little flare of temper died, leaving her even more cold, and her teeth began to chatter.

It seemed a long time before she heard him on the stairs.

She turned on her side, pulling the covers up over her shoulders and closing her eyes, trying to make her breathing slow and even. Anyone would think from the conversation in her little bedroom, and from her end of it especially, that she was an experienced woman of the world and not a quaking mass of nerves and fright.

Perhaps that was what Yves thought—she couldn't blame him if he did! She had given him every reason to think it. Marianne moaned in despair as she heard the hiss of his shower and the pad of his feet across the bedroom floor. Then there was the movement of the bed as he slid between the sheets. Resolutely, she kept her eyes shut, although she knew that the bedside light was still on, it shone through the thin membrane of her eyelids. Perhaps he thought she was asleep, and she wished he would put the light out so that it would be dark and anonymous again as it had been in her bedroom. Things were much easier in the dark.

A minute passed, two, five, and he lay unmoving. Curiosity lured Marianne out of her pose of sleep. She sat upright, hugging the covers to her chin. He was lying on his back, his hands beneath his head, staring unconcernedly at the ceiling.

'When are you going to put that damned light out?' she demanded, her voice shrill with fright and exasperation.

Lazily Yves shifted himself to face her and his arm came about her, heavy and firm, pulling her close to him while with the other hand he calmly forced the sheets from between her fingers and pulled the covers back.

'When I have seen my wife.' His eyes slowly scanned her as if he was commiting each detail to memory.

'What are you looking for?' she muttered, by now shaking with whatever emotion it was that held her. Fear? Excitement? She didn't know. She put a brave face on it. 'Have you looked enough?' she queried sarcastically. 'I haven't got a wooden leg and all my teeth are my own.'

She shivered again. 'It's cold!' It came out as a whimper.

The whimper was choked off as Yves lowered his head, twisting his hands in her hair to tilt her face to his. Marianne forced herself to lie passively, feeling the warmth of his body against her and his hard mouth demanding, forcing a response from her.

'Put out the light, please,' she almost moaned the request.

Later, he switched the light on again and surveyed her tear-stained face.

'I hurt you. Why did you not tell me?'

Marianne muttered something unintelligible.

'You should have told me,' he scowled at her. 'What do you think I am, some sort of animal? From the way you spoke this evening, I thought you were . . . experienced.'

Angrily she turned on him. 'Just because I can speak of some things without fluttering with maidenly modesty there's no reason for you to suppose that I'm. . . .' Her voice fell away. She couldn't think of the right word. 'You know what I mean,' she finished on a defiant note.

'No!' He raised his eyebrows and she received the distinct impression that he was looking at her as though he had never seen her before.

'Go to sleep, *ma mie*,' he murmured, pulling her against him. 'It will be better next time.'

'It didn't last long,' she sighed, 'and it was so pretty. I thought it suited me.'

'Hmmm?' He was half asleep already.

'My nightgown—it *did* suit me, and you ripped it,' she accused, rather surprised to find that she could think about such a mundane thing, such a trumpery thing after her soul-shattering experience.

'Go to sleep,' she was directed. 'I'll buy you another one.'

In the early dawn Marianne woke to a thin, grey world. There was an iron band around her and she struggled out of it to prop herself on one elbow to survey her sleeping husband. Asleep, he looked quite different, more like the Yves of eight years ago. The hard twist had gone from his mouth and now that his eyes were closed she could no longer see the bitter mockery in their depths. He stirred, his hand searching for her, his arm pulling her close. She tried to wriggle away and the arm tightened. There was a warm breath on her cheek just before his mouth found hers—and this time, as he had promised, it was much better. Yves was quite obviously very experienced, and she tried desperately to remain unmoved. She failed miserably and hoped that he had not noticed. She peeped at his sleeping face; the mouth was quiet and contented. With a little sigh of despair she moved closer to him. Life was getting very complicated.

When she had returned, it had been the hazy idea of taking up where she had left off eight years previously. Even knowing that she loved Yves and wanted him was just *knowing*, with no idea of what it would be like. She knew that the experience had changed her, but somewhere at the back of her mind she doubted if Yves would show much change. He would still be hard and cold and . . . suspicious; he would also be insolent and arrogant. He had let her see the old softer side of him so, she suspected, he would be extra hard and cold in order to wipe out the memory from her mind. She would not allow him to wipe it away, not if he went on being bad-tempered and caustic for years! She snuggled a little closer, relaxing and letting her eyes close. She was warm and comfortable and she had been as near to the stars as she was ever likely to get. She would like to stay like this for ever.

A bumping and a rattling awoke her to broad daylight, and she stretched out a hand sleepily to an empty space. Yves had gone and there was a pattering of feet along the corridor. Sylvie pushed open the door with her hip and came across to put a small tray on the bedside table, then with a practised flip she sent the curtains flying back on their rod and stooped to pick up the green nightgown from where it lay on the floor by the bed.

'*Bonjour, madame,*' Sylvie grinned broadly. What a tale she would have to tell when she returned home! A beautiful nightgown ruined! Figuratively, she licked her lips and turned her eyes to Madame Bersac who was lying, as she could see, as naked as the day she was born. So much for the village gossip! Mentally, Sylvie snorted. All those tales Madame Fortin had spread about a marriage of convenience, because Monsieur's old grandmother had wished it, because he wanted La Barrière and would do anything to get it! It all looked perfectly normal to her, and so she would tell the old women who spread such malicious tales. Idly she wondered what Madame would do with the nightgown. Perhaps, if Madame was generous, and it was said that the English were generous to the point of folly, she, Sylvie, could have it. Her mother could repair the trifling tear and with a little adjustment it would fit beautifully. Such silk and such fine lace, obviously of the very finest quality—nobody else would have anything like it! Sylvie drew a deep breath; nothing venture, nothing gained.

'The nightgown, *madame*. You wish it to be repaired invisibly? My mother. . . .'

'Dusters,' came Marianne's somewhat embarrassed voice from the depths of her pillow.

Sylvie turned to go, the nightgown hugged to her young bosom. She could hardly wait for five o'clock when she would go home. She would have a fine tale to tell, with proof, if anybody wanted it. She swelled with importance. She would work very hard all day, then the time would go quickly. Her hands stroked the soft, shimmering silk. Dusters? Never! Not while her name was Sylvie Berthilot!

CHAPTER FOUR

Liz Ross looked across the kitchen of La Barrière at Marianne. It was a look compounded of curiosity and disbelief.

'This isn't you,' she said wonderingly. 'You'll be bored to tears in another six months. I can see it coming.'

'You see what you want to see,' Marianne said forcefully. 'I'm not a bit bored. You forget that this is what I'm used to, what I was brought up to.' She tempered her denial with a warm smile. 'I lived here for over half my life before I came to London. Why should I be bored with the sort of life which I know very well? Nobody forced me to stay here, you know.'

'I'll admit one advantage,' Liz's mouth twisted in wry humour. 'That sexy hunk you're married to.' Her voice dropped to a low register in mimicry of Yves. 'Welcome to La Barrière, *madame*! Why didn't I see him first?' she grieved. 'Some people have all the luck.' Her blue eyes sharpened. 'But going to bed with a man isn't the same as living with him—I should know.'

'Yes, you should,' Marianne's answer came a trifle sardonically.

'Don't blame me,' her friend replied without rancour. 'It's my incurable curiosity. I see a man and I ask myself, is he the one? Can I be happy with him? And I have to find out. The fact that I've tried a few and they've all turned out to be non-starters isn't my fault entirely. I'm looking for one who'll look after me, and what do I keep getting? Little boys who expect me to look after them!' She shook her smooth blonde head.

Standing in the kitchen of La Barrière, Liz was unconsciously an anachronism, nearly as out of place as Mr Gillespie's senior clerk who had come the previous week, a tall, thin, grey-haired man in immaculate pin-striped trousers with a snow-white collar and a symphonic tie peeping between the lapels of his black jacket. He had been very nice, though; he had helped Marianne with the making of a will, brought bank statements and lists of shareholdings and been appreciative of the fresh air and the French farmhouse cooking. Liz wasn't wearing pin-stripe trousers, nor was she soberly dressed. Scarlet woollen trousers, very tight, adorned her petite frame and were topped with a white angora sweater. She was also wearing white high-heeled boots and she had tossed her scarlet reefer jacket down carelessly on a chair. At the skiing resort she was bound for, she would undoubtedly go down a bomb, but she was a little too vivid for La Barrière. Marianne looked at her fondly.

'But you're not happy, are you?' Liz sounded disbelieving. 'You aren't the homespun type, or if you are, I've never seen any evidence of it.'

Marianne turned back from her new gas cooker. 'Who is completely happy, Liz?' she queried gently. 'Not you, not me, not anyone. So stop this soul-searching and come and see your bedroom.' She paused on the stairs. 'It's utilitarian, I'm afraid.' She led the way along the corridor and pushed open the door of the little white room which had once been her own and which she had so lately vacated. 'I haven't started on the upstairs yet, I've been too busy getting the salon and dining room in order—and you're wrong, Liz. I am the homespun type. It didn't show in London, that's all.'

'Convince me!' jeered Liz, her blue eyes sparkling. 'We'll get rid of that beautiful brute of a husband you've collected and we'll have a cosy session of girl talk. You shall tell me all!' She glanced around the room. 'Oh, lord!' Her expression was comical. 'What was this place before you came? A convent? I've never seen such a narrow bed!'

'Quite comfortable, though, I can vouch for it. This used to be my room.' Marianne twitched back the thick white bedspread.

'But you moved out, into his?' Liz slanted a mocking glance upwards. 'Not that I'd blame you, I'd do the same thing myself at the drop of a hat. Talk about machismo!'

'We are married,' Marianne said in a reproving tone.

'And he's satisfactory? Makes your little heart go pit-a-pat and all that sort of thing?'

Marianne chuckled. 'Oh yes, he's very satisfactory.' Her lips curved in a reminiscent smile and Liz hooted with laughter.

'Wait till I tell them back home!' Her eyes sparkled with derision. 'Marianne, our ice maiden, has defrosted, melted, gone all slushy. They'll never believe me—I hardly believe it myself. The iceberg turned into a warm pool!' Her eyes sharpened. 'It's all right, isn't it?' Her lively little face had a faint look of worry.

'Quite all right.' Marianne injected a firm note of assurance into her reply. 'It couldn't be better.' She wasn't telling lies, she told herself, Yves was a very satisfactory husband in one way at least. It was as though he had been starving for a very long time. 'I've no complaints at all.' There was a note in her voice which forbade further questions on the subject.

Over breakfast next morning, a cosy coffee and croissants affair with Sylvie busy in the salon clearing up the evidence of what could only be termed as a convivial evening, Marianne attempted to explain why Serac Ste. Marie was not the same as the jet-set resorts in the south of France. Liz was bemused. 'But it's all France, isn't it?' she demanded.

'Idiot!' Marianne grinned at her. 'You can't call Nice and St Tropez France. They're artificial places for the tourist trade. This is France. No tourists to be catered for or pampered here, this is the real thing, the real provincial France. That village down there,' she nodded out of the window, 'it's just the same as any other village anywhere else in the world. It's like trying to say that Southend is typical of England.'

'Well, it is,' Liz wrinkled her brow.

'It's typical of an English resort,' argued Marianne, 'but it's nothing like Nether Wallop, is it?'

'I see what you mean. There's that little village in Sussex, everyone's related to everyone else, it's a hotbed of gossip, but let a stranger put a foot wrong and the whole lot come down on you like a ton of bricks.'

'Exactly!' Marianne grimaced. 'Serac Ste. Marie is just like Nether Wallop.' Liz came to stand by her and look down at the small steep-sided valley with its huddle of houses strung out around the church. It was in plain view now that winter had stripped the leaves from the trees and the bare branches no longer provided the screen that they gave in summer. 'There's just the same avarice, love and hate down there as there is in any other village anywhere else in the world. But like any other village, it's all covered up. Everyone knows all about it, but they all pretend that it isn't there. English villages are like that too, aren't they?'

'The one I know is,' Liz grimaced. 'You get the idea after a while that they all hate each other like mad, but scratch one of them and they rise in a body to repel invaders.'

'Same here,' Marianne smiled. 'That's why it's not like Cannes or Biarritz. See the difference now? That whole place is a hotbed of gossip. Nothing about the villagers themselves, you understand. Their own little peccadilloes are tactfully smoothed over, if a man has a little friend around the corner, they all know about it but nobody ever mentions it—but let someone from outside put one foot wrong and the tongues start wagging.'

'And does that sexy husband of yours have a little friend

around the corner?' Liz's patrician little nose quivered like that of a hound catching the scent and her eyes gleamed very blue.

Marianne shrugged gracefully. 'What a question to ask about a newly married man! If that sort of thing ever happened, it wouldn't be anyone in the village, I can assure you of that. They, some of them,' she gestured disdainfully towards the distant roofs, 'they call him a murderer.'

'A murderer?' Liz let it out as a yelp. 'That does it! You're coming with me and you're coming now. We'll go and pack your things. . . .'

'Don't be foolish.' Marianne found herself smiling. 'He's no such thing. I wouldn't have married him if I'd thought that.' Or would she have? She didn't know. Hastily she explained, 'His first wife was a village girl, they didn't get on and one day she stormed out saying that she was leaving. She took a little old Fiat van they had for farm work and drove it off. It crashed on the hill and she was killed. Later the whispering started. Somebody suggested that the brakes had been tampered with. In no time at all, it was all over the village; not out loud and not on the surface, you understand. That was as smooth as a millpond, but it was all there underneath, and our marriage hasn't made it any better. I don't worry too much about it, nor about the silly tales that people tell each other. Most of their lives are very drab, I suppose they appreciate a bit of excitement now and then, especially if it happens to somebody else, there's a certain fillip in being able to talk about it. Yves stalks through it untouched, I think he's trained himself not to notice, but I find myself watching.'

At that moment the telephone shrilled from the office and leaving Liz looking out of the window, Marianne went to answer it. Tante Monique's voice came over the wire, the tones almost honeyed. She and Bernard wanted to see Yves, a matter of business but a good excuse for a social call. Families must stick together and more than that, be seen to stick together. Did Marianne agree with her?

Marianne muttered something unintelligible and Tante continued like a circular saw cutting through a plank. She and Bernard would come for dinner this evening and afterwards the little business deal could be aired.

'We already have a visitor.' Marianne glared at the mouthpiece.

Yes, Tante knew of the visitor, a friend of Marianne's from London, was it not? This would be a most agreeable opportunity to meet a friend of Marianne.

Marianne did a quick mental flip through the refrigerator and decided on a trip to Rémy. It would be quicker, of course, to go down to the village where she could obtain everything she needed in the way of meat from Bernard's shop, but if she did that, Tante would have something to say about a woman who could not whip up a gorgeous meal for five out of nothing at a moment's notice. Besides, she felt a curious reluctance to go into Bernard's shop. She couldn't very well be disagreeable over Tante and Bernard's visit either. They were Yves's relations and one day she would have to invite them, so she might just as well get it over and done with.

'Can you drive me down to Rémy?' she asked Liz. 'We're going to have visitors tonight, relatives of Yves. It will give you a chance to meet the locals,' she added with a sideways smile. 'Yves's aunt and his cousin Bernard have invited themselves for dinner and there's some business involved as well. I can't very well put them off, so I'm going to need some extra meat and a few other things.'

Liz had returned downstairs and was busy eating the rest of the croissants and helping herself to more coffee. 'Just give me five minutes, sit down and have another cup of coffee yourself. What do we wear tonight? Do we wow them with glamour or would something more restrained be better?'

'Glamour would be wasted on Tante Monique, although you'd probably make Bernard dribble.' Marianne was thoughtful. 'I think we should try for the elegant look. You'll be all right, but I shall need all the confidence I can get, most of my clothes are still in London. We'll choose after we get back from Rémy. It's a little less than an hour's drive and I'll leave word with Sylvie before we go, then if Yves should come home for lunch, she can put him in the picture.'

Liz hurled the Triumph TR7 around corners and up and down hills with abandon, but Marianne sat unmoved through the hair-raising experience. Liz's husband had been a well-known racing driver and he had taught Liz well. Liz had loved him with a one-off type of love and his death on a racing circuit had left her brittle and with an emptiness that she feverishly tried to fill. An aching void had been left in her life when Jimmy Ross had perished in the blazing sunlight of a race-track in Mexico.

'Chicken, I think, with mushrooms and a cream sauce, haricots verts and a side salad and finish it with an apple charlotte with cream,' Marianne mused aloud, and Liz nodded vehemently as she parked the car.

'Sounds wonderful to me. I haven't had a decent meal at home since you took off for France.' Liz was bent on poking her small, straight nose into every nook and cranny of Rémy. 'Part of my charm,' she laughed at Marianne's severe look. 'People like other people to be interested in them. What's the use of wearing an outsize diamond if nobody asks "Is that real?" or wearing your very latest clothes if nobody says how lovely they are? We will now go to the butcher's shop and I shall tell you how lovely everything looks, and then he'll sell you the best chickens.'

'Have you bought everything you need?' Liz executed a neat sidestep to avoid a little girl carrying an armful of baguettes. She looked askance at Marianne's bulging shopping bag. 'Because if you have, I'm going to look for something to wear. I saw a shop backaways and the window looked chic.'

Madame Jeanne produced her wares after a critical survey of her two customers. For Liz, she produced a long white wool smock with a hint of scarlet embroidery around the neckline. Liz cooed and danced around the fitting room. 'V-e-r-y nice,' she crooned. 'Now let's see what she can find for you.'

Marianne demurred, she had enough, and Liz groaned with displeasure. 'You can never have enough! Come on, Madame Jeanne, you've got something tucked away for Madame Bersac, haven't you?'

Madame Jeanne reminded Marianne that she had searched for a long dress for her and then brought out the results of her search. She carried it over her arm with the same pride with which she would have exhibited had it been a Medal of the Legion of Honour. It was a dark green gown that glittered softly with gold embroidery, and Liz leapt upon it. 'The very thing, all loose and elegant. That'll set your brute back on his heels!'

It was impossible to resist Liz in this mood. Marianne had known her friend too long to try, and the two girls went back to the car laden with their booty and vastly pleased with themselves.

Yves's face that evening was a mask of non-expression. He might have been glad of the company or he might have been seething with disapproval, it was impossible to say.

Marianne sat in front of the mirror in their bedroom and did things to her face, things she hadn't bothered about all the time she had been in France, except on her wedding day. She had examined her features carefully and she thought that she did not look so very different. It didn't show, this peculiar marriage of hers. She looked very much as she always had.

When she had finished with her face, her eyes were a definite green, her mouth softly red and her skin looked like cream. Her pale red hair had been brushed and coiled into a smooth, loose chignon and fastened with a couple of gilt-headed pins. The new gown drifted around her like a dream, just covering the tips of her gilt, high-heeled sandals. She was very pleased with herself and she hoped that Tante Monique was not going to spoil her pleasure with one of her flattening remarks.

Tante and Bernard arrived promptly at seven. Bernard's mother was wearing a highly coloured purple dress. On somebody slimmer and of a paler complexion, it might have looked good, but it made Tante Monique look as if she was on the verge of apoplexy. Bernard followed behind his mother as if he was attached to her with an invisible cord and his flat wet eyes looked over Liz with something hot lurking in their shallow depths. To Marianne, it looked very much like lust, and she remembered that Bernard had always liked blondes. Tante, she decided, kept him on too short a leading rein.

Evidently Liz felt the same, for she whispered *sotto voce*, 'Hungry little thing, isn't he?'

Yves poured pre-dinner sherry in the salon, bringing Marianne hers in the kitchen where she was busy making the sauce for the chicken.

'You should have kept Sylvie on,' he scowled. 'I don't like this thing on you.' He gave a little tug to the wide white tapes which held her apron about her, and Marianne looked at him in astonishment.

'Sylvie's hours are agreed, and besides, she had a date tonight. She's been looking forward to it all week—I couldn't disappoint her. It wouldn't have made much difference anyway, I'd not have left the making of a sauce to her.'

'Your friend Liz,' his face looked sombre, 'she is very lively.'

'Yes, isn't she marvellous?' Marianne heard herself babbling. 'You'd never think that she misses her husband so much. That's what all the feverish gaiety is about, you know. He was a racing driver and he was killed nearly four years ago.' She turned to him, her face serious. 'Don't judge her too harshly, Yves. She loved him very much and it's mostly grief and loneliness that make her glitter. She's looking all the time for a substitute. I know how hard she was hit, I was with her when the news came in.'

'Having been judged myself, *madame*,' Yves made it very formal, 'I would not sit in judgment on anybody.'

Marianne's face flamed at the implied rebuke and she swallowed her sherry hastily. How could she have been so stupid? Yves was incapable of being petty. She thought of Tante, sitting in Yves's house, drinking his wine and eating his food and condemning him with every second word she uttered, yet he remained courteous.

'Go back to the salon,' she urged him. 'I'm nearly finished here, I'm just going to carry the dishes through to the dining room.'

Dinner was an awkward meal. Tante and Bernard spoke no English and Liz's French was of the hit or miss variety, mostly miss. More than that, Yves had very little to say and Marianne feared she would get a severe headache, continually translating from one language to another; it made for stilted conversation, and it was with a definite sense of relief that she learned that Tante and Bernard were both to go into the office with Yves. As Bernard's mother pointed out, the discussion had nothing to do with Madame Ross, she turned a wooden smile on Liz; and of course Marianne would wish to stay with her friend.

'And she can't wait to remove her son from my corrupting influence,' Liz giggled. 'Not that she has anything to fear, I wouldn't touch him with a bargepole, he gives me the shivers. Besides, he's not really interested in me.' She looked sideways at Marianne. 'He might want to give that impression, but he's got his eyes firmly fixed on you. He practically dribbles when he looks at you. Hasn't your beautiful brute noticed it yet? There's not much gets by that one.'

Finally, Tante and Bernard left amid a cloud of Tante's Eastern Promise perfume. Bernard smiled beautifully and dutifully while his mother promised them the pleasure of her company again as soon as she could fit them in with her roster of dinner engagements and duty visits. When they had at last gone, Yves suggested that they all return to the salon to sample a bottle of wine which he had been saving for just such an occasion.

'Just one glass,' Liz grinned at him in an uninhibited way, 'then a couple of pills and I'm off to bed. Dinner was gorgeous,' she told Marianne. 'I don't know how you do it.'

After Liz had gone, Yves refilled Marianne's glass. He had turned out the central cluster of lights and the golden liquid shimmered in the light from the table lamp. Marianne felt pleasantly tired and relaxed on the couch, supporting her head with one hand. Her first dinner party in her own home, and it had gone off very well. The food had been good and well cooked and the new curtains in the dining room and the salon had cut out a lot of draughts.

Yves—she turned to look at him. After his aunt and cousin had left, he had thawed considerably; she had even seen him smile. How long would it take, she wondered idly, for the thawing process to get down to his heart, or would that lie forever buried under a layer of permafrost? Was it so frozen that nothing could ever make it warm again? Unconsciously her eyes closed. The warmth of the fire, the wine and the satisfaction of feeling well fed, were all making her drowsy.

'Bed for you, *ma mie*,' Yves's voice jerked her awake. 'And there is no need for you to rise early in the morning. Sylvie can see to the breakfast.'

'But there's a mountain of washing up,' she protested. 'I can't leave all that to Sylvie.'

'Sylvie will cope, it is what she is paid to do. You have other duties, Marianne.'

Still drowsy, she blinked at him, 'What duties?'

Gently he pushed her towards the staircase. 'A stupid question, and one that I shall not bother to answer.' He closed the bedroom door on them and Marianne shivered. It was much colder upstairs and she regretted having to leave the warmth of the salon.

'A shiver?' He was sardonic. 'What brought that about? Fright, distaste or the cold, *madame*?'

Marianne stood in her long slip, the green gown in her hands, ready to be hung in the wardrobe. 'I'm not frightened of you, Yves, nor do I find you distasteful, so it must be the cold. More than that I can't say.'

'You've said enough!' Heavens above—he was laughing at her, and she caught her breath. Yves actually laughing!

'Go and wash your face,' he told her. 'You'll soon be warm in bed.'

Once in bed, his hands found her, arousing her, and his mouth teased. Marianne was in no mood to be teased. She was filled with a strange longing and she seized his head in firm hands, dragging it down to her own and thrusting herself closer to him. It was the first time that she had ever tried to tempt him and she hoped desperately that she would succeed, because if she didn't, she didn't know what else to do. She heard his laugh on a breath come softly, triumph and approval together in it, and she sighed with relief. She was learning something new each day. Dimly she thought, Bernard isn't the only one that's hungry, Yves is hungry too—and then she stopped thinking and became lost in a mindless bliss.

The next day Yves explained the so secret business. Bernard had an idea for the bulk supply of meat for deep freezers. Yves would supply the cattle, sheep and pigs,

Bernard would butcher and sell, and the profits would be equally shared between them.

Marianne wrinkled her brow thoughtfully. 'Capital expenditure,' she mused aloud. 'Bernard will have to increase his cold storage facilities and invest in a larger van. Deep freezers don't exactly bloom like the flowers in May, not in Serac Ste. Marie, so Bernard will have to go farther afield for customers. You could be rearing cattle and feeding them without any guarantee of sale.' She explained as well as she could. 'To get as much business as possible, Bernard will have to establish a clientele in the rural areas, which would mean a lot of travelling, and travelling's expensive.'

She did not like to say that her disinclination for Yves to work with Bernard was based on the fact that she did not like Bernard and she automatically suspected any scheme he tried to involve Yves in. He would have to come up to La Barrière more frequently, and that was something she did not want.

'Bernard is a slimy little creep,' she concluded, looking at Yves to see if he was offended at her valuation of his cousin, but her husband's face was set in an enigmatic mask. 'I don't like him and I don't want him here any more than is strictly necessary. I don't trust him,' she ended darkly.

Liz, who had been an interested listener, broke in. 'Listen to her! Anyone would think your cousin's a ravening wolf bent on destroying you.' She turned back from Yves to Marianne. 'Don't over-dramatise, Marianne. It's a good business deal—my father had the same sort of thing going in Somerset about five years ago, and he made a packet before he sold out.'

'Liz is right.' Yves sounded bewildered. 'What is this with you, *ma mie*? Never have I found you reluctant to consider a business proposition, especially one which has more than a good chance of success.' He smiled at Liz.

'Would you believe it, Liz? This is the girl who wished me to buy a tractor or a piece of land instead of a betrothal ring!' He turned back to his wife. 'You have no need to fear, *ma mie*. It will be gone into very carefully, costed and so on. I am not a fool.'

Liz and Yves went on talking, mostly about the bulk selling of meat for deep freezers. Marianne listened to them for a short while, thinking that Yves was hiding his surprise very well. For a person who didn't look able to add two and two together and get the right answer, Liz was displaying a surprising knowledge of business. Perhaps, though, Yves wasn't surprised, perhaps he had evaluated Liz much more realistically than the majority of men who thought of her as a typical dumb blonde. Then she turned once more to the business on hand while she kept her eyes on the flames leaping from the logs on the fire.

'I still don't like it,' she said stubbornly. 'Any other partner and I'd be all in favour, but Bernard—uggh!' She grasped the coffee pot. 'Anyone want more coffee?' There must be something wrong with her, she decided. She could raise no enthusiasm for the project. To her it was simply a means Tante Monique and Bernard were using to get inside her house. Marianne smiled to herself. *Her* house! She was getting obsessive about it.

Three days later Liz left for the unpronounceable town in Switzerland where she intended to spend Christmas skiing and living the high life. Marianne watched the scarlet and cream TR7 out of sight, then turned back to the house.

Half an hour later she watched as Bernard drove his van into the yard. There, she had been right! It had started already. Eyes sparking green with temper, she met Bernard at the kitchen door.

'Yves isn't home,' she said shortly, standing in the doorway like Horatius defending the bridge. Bernard would have to push her aside to get into the house, and she didn't think he'd do that. His round, boyish features creased with disappointment.

'But I wanted to see him, we have so much to discuss. Perhaps I could wait. . . .' He looked so much like a schoolboy denied a treat that she relented.

'Yves said he would be back within the hour, and that was more than half an hour ago. You can wait for him in here.' She stepped aside to let him go past her into the kitchen. 'But I warn you, if he's not back by lunchtime, I shan't expect him before dinner time tonight and it will be quite useless for you to wait.' She went and seated herself in the cane armchair, waving him to a straight-backed one. He did not take it, however, but came to stand beside her.

'Marianne, you do not know, you can have no conception of how much I worry about you, alone here with Yves. He has had a great deal to bear and God knows, I have always tried to see the best in everybody, especially my relatives, but there have been times when I have doubted Yves's sanity.'

Her mouth made a round 'O' of shocked surprise, but that was all. Her voice, when it came, was cool and indifferent. 'You're being quite ridiculous! Doubting Yves's sanity indeed! Surely if you feel that way, you shouldn't be so ready to do business with him.' Marianne tilted her chin and looked at Bernard with dislike. 'If you want to hold a conversation on those lines, you can hold it by yourself and with yourself, out in your van. I don't want to have any part of it.'

'But, Marianne, *ma petite*. . . .'

Marianne spoilt this intentionally. She rose to her feet. When she did this, her eyes were on a level with Bernard's. 'I am not your *petite*!' By this time anger had crept into her voice, sharpening it. 'And I've no desire to be your *petite*.' She looked scornful. 'You've a business deal going with Yves, so stick to it,' she advised him harshly. 'There's room for one man in this house and one man only, and that man is Yves. I neither need nor want your concern so you are wasting your time. Go and bleat to your *maman* if you must bleat to anyone, she'll listen to you, perhaps. I won't, and you can't make me!' Stormily, she went to the door that led into the hall and fumbled for the knob. 'If you want to wait for Yves, you can do it on your own. I have work to do.'

Marianne swished out in high dudgeon. The little creep, she thought, and then a reluctant smile curved her lips. He was bound to be a creep, wasn't he? Anybody with a mother like Tante Monique would be!

Sylvie was putting the finishing touches to the salon and Marianne looked around with a satisfied smile. She had done a good job on this room, she congratulated herself. Even on a cold, grey day like today, it looked warm and pleasant, not a bit like the stiff greeny-grey it had been formerly. There was no place for Gisèle here now!

By mutual consent she and Sylvie went into the dining-room. There wasn't much to do in there, but Marianne was looking for work which would keep her out of the kitchen, so she decided that the table needed to be polished. Sylvie trotted back to the kitchen for her polishing cloths.

'Monsieur Fortin sits alone in the kitchen,' she murmured when she returned. 'He looks agitated.'

'Leave him, Sylvie, forget he's there.' Marianne spread polish on the dining table. 'He came to see Monsieur Yves on business and we cannot help him.' And we wouldn't if we could, she added silently.

Sylvie nodded energetically. 'But it is strange to see him once more at La Barrière after all this time,' she muttered. 'Before the accident to the first Madame Bersac, he was often here, but afterwards he did not come any more.'

'He used to come to see Madame Gisèle?' Marianne could not hide the surprise she felt and the words had escaped her without any conscious volition on her part. She was sorry almost as soon as she had said them. Sylvie tapped the side of her nose and looked wise.

'Me, I was a child still, at school, but often we would see Monsieur Fortin's car come up here. Sometimes he would walk up the hill. We knew about it even though we were only children, you understand? We knew where they went.' She giggled at a hilarious thought. 'Jacques—you know Jacques, *madame*, he works for Monsieur Yves with the machinery on the farm and down at the vineyard—Jacques had to sit all one afternoon in a walnut tree because they were underneath it.'

Marianne took a deep breath and continued polishing with increased vigour. 'You must not gossip, Sylvie,' she lectured sternly. 'Sometimes things are misunderstood and to gossip about them makes trouble. It is detraction, and I don't think that the *curé* would like that.'

'But we did not gossip, *madame*.' Sylvie managed to look hurt and virtuous at one and the same time. 'It was our secret, mine and Jacques. We spoke of it only to each other. I did not even tell my mother.'

Mechanically polishing, Marianne forced her mind away from the subject of Bernard and concentrated on other things. Sylvie's bright chatter became a pleasant background noise as she mentally visualised the bedrooms and tried to decide what she was going to do about them. Pastel colours, she thought, and fitted furniture in the smaller rooms. That would give their narrow confines a more spacious air. Muslin curtains against the windows and heavier ones to draw across, soft carpeting and gay rugs, anything to remove the monastic air about which Liz had been so scathing.

In the middle of trying to decide whether she would have the floors carpeted or not, she heard the slam of the back door into the kitchen. That would be either Yves coming in or Bernard leaving, tired of waiting. Either happening would be welcome. Marianne stood back to admire the gleam of polish on the table top and after making sure that there were no dull patches or smears on the shining surface, she folded her dusters and returned to the kitchen. Bernard was still there, sitting at the table, and Yves was shrugging himself out of his sheepskin coat.

'Bernard has been waiting for you for nearly half an hour,' she remarked brightly as she passed her husband to wash her hands at the sink.

Yves spared a glance for his cousin before he bent his head to bestow a totally unexpected kiss on his wife's mouth. Marianne, her hands wet and soapy, was startled by this unaccustomed display of affection. It was utterly unlike Yves to make any public display of his feelings, and she concluded that he was intent on giving Bernard a very false impression of the state of affairs at La Barrière. Her eyes narrowed and deliberately she raised a wet, soapy hand and stroked his cheek with it. 'That'll teach you,' she murmured in English, meanwhile giving him a smile of syrupy sweetness before she whisked herself off to the range where her pot-au-feu was giving off mouthwatering odours.

Yves followed her and put his arm around her in a competent fashion and quite deliberately bit her ear. Marianne stood still for a moment within his arm and gave what she hoped was a gay laugh, then she pushed him away.

'Wash before lunch,' she told him, 'and do change that jacket, it smells as though you've been to bed with some calves! Hurry, darling,' once more she smiled artificially. 'Bernard wants to talk business and he's been waiting long enough.'

Hastily she laid the table. She slapped soup bowls on the top crossly and brought out bread, cheese and a large bowl of salad. It wasn't that she minded Yves kissing her, she liked it very much. It was his motives that made her angry. Kissing her just to give Bernard an impression of marital bliss, sweetness, light and love evermore was laying it on a bit too thick. She began to fill soup bowls and forgave herself her little rage. She and Yves met only in bed, to their mutual satisfaction she had to admit, but apart from that, they might just as well have been two strangers forced to share a house. And it wasn't her fault, she decided crossly. It was Yves who kept himself remote, wouldn't soften, insisted on staying suspicious.

When he came back from the bathroom she gave him what might very well pass for a loving smile, and then Sylvie came running to join them and Marianne felt positively elated. Bernard wouldn't be able to discuss any business with Sylvie seated beside him, her ears pricked for any little particle of information which would serve to entertain her mother that evening. A wasted journey, in fact, and Marianne's eyes gleamed green with satisfaction until she realised that it would mean that Bernard would, in all probability, call again in the evening.

CHAPTER FIVE

MARIANNE sat and toasted her toes before the fire in the salon, staring gloomily at the flames that licked around the logs. Yves had brought this load of wood in from the orchard where he had been cutting down some of the old trees to make room for new stock. The apple logs burned with a clear flame and did not spit, and Marianne liked to think she could smell the scent of apples as they burned. They were piled high in the grate, the clear yellow flames licking around the grey bark of the topmost logs. One, half consumed, fell with a soft hiss and a shower of sparks, and Marianne stirred herself to bend and brush the feathery ash from the tiles of the hearth.

Yves was stuck in the office with Bernard again; it was

quite a usual occurrence nowadays. Marianne glanced at her watch and sniffed as she thought of them in there. Yves would be patiently explaining some point which Bernard could not or would not grasp and the number of points about which Bernard wanted clarification was legion. The business sessions became longer each time.

Just occasionally, Tante Monique accompanied her son, which meant that Marianne had equally long sessions with her aunt-in-law in the salon, something she disliked very much. There was no common ground between the two women, so there was nothing for them to talk about. Not that she would have been given the opportunity to talk, Marianne reflected dismally. Tante did not need another person in order to hold a conversation—she did not hold conversations, only monologues! She stated her opinions forcefully and with vigour and was quite unable to understand anyone even wanting to disagree with her.

This evening, fortunately, Bernard had come by himself, inviting himself for dinner and after the meal, going directly to the office with Yves so that there had been no chance for Marianne to have a word with her husband either before, during or after the meal, and Marianne wanted to get the ban on driving removed. It was now just a little less than a month before Christmas and Marianne, naturally, had a few little ideas about Christmas.

In the French fashion, Yves made more of St Nicholas's Day, but Marianne, after eight years in England, was not going to neglect her English friends. They were going to receive cards and gifts from her at the correct time. There were presents to be bought and she had been looking forward to buying them, choosing gifts for each and every one of her small circle of friends. There was something very nice about a well wrapped parcel and French goods were always prettily packaged, but to get them, she had to go either to Rémy or to Clermont-Ferrand, and as she intended using her own money, she wanted to go by herself. That meant using the Mini, and Yves had forbidden her to drive anywhere.

Her train of thought was broken by the entrance of Yves and Bernard, who came into the salon at that moment. Her eyes went first to Yves's face; he was looking harassed and his lips, set in a straight line, betokened temper. Bernard, on the other hand, positively oozed satisfaction.

'Marianne,' he clasped her hand as if it was something precious. 'We have not kept you up too late, I hope. There are so many things, so many preliminaries before we can even start to make definite arrangements and to discuss one thing leads on to another automatically.' His air was of ingratiating good humour and Marianne had a wild desire to box his ears. Clasping her hands together tightly, she restrained the impulse and merely enquired if either of them wanted coffee. Yves made no reply to her question and Bernard refused.

'I have kept you from your bed long enough,' he said with what Marianne decided was almost a leer.

'You can say that again,' she muttered in English while smiling brightly and glaring at the brass carriage clock that stood on the mantlepiece. It was gone eleven o'clock and Yves would be up again at the crack of dawn, so she would have no time to get the driving ban lifted tonight!

Bernard, having said that he must go immediately, delayed his departure for about another half hour while Marianne yawned pointedly. Nothing can last for ever, she comforted herself and fixed a smile on her lips that remained there until Bernard finally made his way through the door and out into the cold winter night. Yves patiently escorted him to the van and Marianne laid bets with herself as to how long Bernard would keep Yves hanging about in the cold.

When Yves came back, she was in the kitchen preparing a pot of coffee.

'What did he want this time?' she enquired with exasperation.

'Clarification. You do not like my little cousin, Marianne?'

'No, I don't.' She set the coffee pot down with a thump. 'As far as I'm concerned, Bernard's all right as long as he's kept in his place, and that's down in Serac in his butcher's shop. I don't want him up here.' She poured two cups of coffee and pushed one across to Yves. 'Cognac?' she asked briefly, and at his nod, went to fetch the bottle and glasses from the salon.

'I wonder why you do not like our little Bernard?' He poured small quantities of the golden liquid into two glasses. 'He is very well liked in the village.'

Marianne pushed distracted fingers through her hair. 'It's too late for soul-searching tonight. I don't like Bernard, let's leave it at that. Call it antipathy if you like.' Then irritation got the better of her and the question she had been wanting to ask all evening popped out before she could stop it. 'Yves, when are you going to let me drive my Mini? It's going to fall into a heap of rust if it's left in the barn much longer, and I need it. I could do my Christmas shopping without having to drag you away from your work.'

'Have I complained?' He leaned back lazily in his chair, the heavy lids nearly closed over his eyes.

'No, you haven't,' she admitted grudgingly, 'but. . . .'

'Then, until I do complain, why make a fuss?' He rose to his feet. 'Come to bed, Marianne, it is too late to start even a small quarrel about the Mini. Tomorrow we will talk about it, hmm?'

Marianne's laugh was decidedly cynical. 'What's the betting that Bernard doesn't find another five hundred points to clarify and takes up all your time tomorrow evening?'

'What gave you that pessimistic thought?'

'It's not a pessimistic thought,' Marianne said tartly as

she went before him up the stairs. 'It's getting to be standard practice!'

Two days later she gleefully drove the Mini down the hill to Serac on her way to Rémy. Yves was away all day, visiting a farmer in Brive, and as soon as the Citroën had disappeared down the hill, she had sent Sylvie scurrying to find Jacques.

'Check the Mini for me, please,' she smiled winningly. 'I want to go to Rémy today.'

'But, *madame*, Monsieur Yves. . . .' Marianne swore under her breath. Did everyone know about the ban on her driving?

'Monsieur Yves is away in Brive today,' she smiled at Jacques and Sylvie, 'and I shall be home soon after lunch. Check the car please, Jacques. It's been standing in the barn a long time. Monsieur would not like me to use it without making sure it was in good order.'

Jacques was obliging, he checked the oil, brakes, steering and the lights and finally handed it over to her.

'It is in very good condition, *madame*,' he told her, looking at the little car wistfully. 'If it was properly tuned, it would do many more kilometres per hour.'

Marianne hesitated, then, 'Monsieur Yves and I have thought of replacing it with a more serviceable vehicle—a Land Rover perhaps. If you didn't find the right-hand drive uncomfortable, perhaps you would like. . . .' She got no further. Sylvie was at her back, squealing with delight.

'We have some small savings, *madame*.' Her young face was eager and she launched into a flood of the local patois to which Jacques listened with smiling reserve.

'Speak to Monsieur about it,' Marianne recommended as she drove off.

The steepness of the hill and the hairpin bends worried her not one jot. It was a bright frosty day and it was good to be driving again. As she passed over the bridge into Serac, she spared a glance for the tumbling water it spanned. It seemed higher than when she had seen it last, but the Massif Central was a good watershed and the rain which had been falling steadily all through November to the south of the Puy de Dome was finding its way into the little rivers and streams that flowed out from it, swelling them, making them rumble through their narrow-cut channels and toss over the rocks that lay in their path.

Just over the bridge, her speed was slowed to a walking pace by two large white geese which had decided to take a morning stroll through the village. They had spaced themselves so that it was impossible to pass them without running down either bird, so Marianne adjusted her speed to their stately waddling gait. Nothing, she knew, would hurry the birds, and she crawled along behind them, listening to the leathery slap of their feet on the road surface and having, for the first time, the leisure to observe some of the changes which had taken place in the village during the eight years of her absence.

Several of the older, smaller cottages had vanished and the *quincaillerie* sported a new façade and a window full of beautiful cooking ware and electrical goods, toasters, table lamps, irons and hairdryers. Serac, she observed, was moving into the twentieth century at last—slowly and with reluctance, but it was moving.

The pavement outside the *bistro* was clear of the little tables and chairs which stood there during the summer months and the colourful awning had been stowed away for the winter. There was a delicious smell from the *pâtisserie* and halfway down the street she caught sight of a muffled-up male figure waving her down. Bernard! Just her luck to encounter him as she was following two geese. She could, of course, wave back and continue without stopping, and for one moment she was tempted to do just that, but inherent good manners prevented her.

She drew the Mini to a halt alongside the narrow pavement and wound the window down. Bernard, from the depths of an enormous scarf wound twice around his neck, wished her 'good morning' and enquired as to the possibility of having a lift into Rémy.

'My van,' he smiled apologetically. 'It won't start this morning—a flat battery, I think, although one can never be certain. And I have been waiting for more than half an hour.' He bundled himself into the front passenger seat. 'I did not hope to be so fortunate as to find somebody going to Rémy at this hour in the morning. Tuesday is not a good day, people prefer to go on Thursday, market day, and the bus service is deplorable.' Here Bernard's face puckered with sorrow. 'I have a most important meeting with Monsieur Matheus at the bank. I was afraid I would have to cancel it and that would upset all my plans.' He brightened visibly. 'But you are here and you are going to Rémy—I shall be forever in your debt.'

Marianne thought of telling him how he might repay that debt. Something like only having weekly meetings with Yves, or possibly fortnightly ones! She glanced at her watch—half past ten; she would make Rémy easily by half past eleven, and that would be more than enough of Bernard for one day, she decided grimly. Especially as he would almost certainly be calling tonight for more clarification. His arm was along the back of her seat and her brows drew together in a scowl. There wasn't much room in a Mini, but there was no need for them to be driving along with Bernard practically hugging her.

She sat upright and concentrated on her driving while her frown gave way to a small smile of unholy glee. Liz had taught her to drive, Liz who had learned from an expert and had passed on a great deal of that expertise to her friend. Marianne could go into a perfectly controlled skid at any turn in the road, if she wanted to. A small twist of her hands, a little pressure on the accelerator followed by a swift stamp on the brake pedal and the Mini rolled alarmingly.

'Better put on your safety belt,' she pointed to the harness. 'There are patches of ice on the road, it will be safer if you're strapped in.'

'But you are not wearing your belt,' Bernard shouted above the wheel noise and the buffeting wind.

'Behind this?' Marianne tapped the steering column. 'No, thank you very much! If we hit anything, I don't want to be tied in behind the steering column. It can go right through you, didn't you know?' She managed another rear wheel skid on the next bend in the road and observed that Bernard's round features were now a pasty yellow and covered with a thin film of perspiration. She went through her full repertoire of sideways slips in a thoroughly heartless manner. Not very comfortable for the passenger, but, she consoled herself, he had to keep his hands to himself!

Bernard descended from the Mini outside the bank, perspiring freely and mopping himself with a handkerchief soaked in attar of roses. Marianne took a delighted sniff. 'Oh, Bernard,' she muttered to herself, 'Monsieur Matheus is going to just *love* you!'

'If my business is completed in time, Marianne, will you have lunch with me?'

'Thank you, but no.' Marianne had her day planned out and it did not include dalliance with Bernard over a lunch table. 'I have to see the plumber, the builder and the little man who's making some furniture for me in his spare time. I'm going to skip lunch today. Au revoir,' and she sent the Mini forging ahead through the streets of Rémy.

Later, her travellers' cheques all spent and her arms full of parcels, she made her way back to the middle of the small town, to the Mini. She released her breath on a groan at the sight of Bernard leaning on the bonnet.

'I have been waiting only a few minutes.' The boyish beam lit his face, all but his eyes which, to Marianne, never seemed anything but flat and hard except when they were lit by a hot gleam. 'It was comparatively simple to find your car, it is the only one of its kind in Rémy.' Marianne thought longingly of a nice inconspicuous Renault or a little Citroën 2CV and swore beneath her breath. She had no excuse, her shopping was all done down to the last piece of wrapping paper and the last roll of sticky tape, and there was nothing for it but to open the door for Bernard.

The last thing she wanted on this homeward journey was company, Bernard's especially. He would chat and she would be expected to listen, even made an intelligent remark now and then. How could she do that when her mind was totally given over to the coming quarrel with Yves?

He was going to lay down the law, in no uncertain terms. He had forbidden her to drive and as soon as his back was turned, she had had the Mini on the road. He was going to be livid, and she had been looking forward to a quiet drive home during which she could rehearse her speeches, think up some cutting remarks and at least have some sort of defence ready.

Bernard enlivened the first few miles with the latest news of Serac and then he approached the theme of frozen meat. Marianne listened with less than half an ear to Bernard's plans; they were grandiose if the places he mentioned meant anything. He was talking of the whole Puy de Dome area down as far as Condat and westward to Port les Orgues.

She hardly noticed the shift in subject matter until the words La Barrière and Gisèle were uttered. Brenard was talking about Gisèle the beautiful, Gisèle the misunderstood, Gisèle who was warm and loving and who had found nothing of warmth or love at la Barrière. Marianne found the pressure of her foot on the accelerator increasing and with a jerk brought the Mini back to a steady thirty miles an hour.

'I knew Gisèle,' she said flatly, as she had said it to his mother.

'Ah, but Marianne, consider. You were a child at the time and your views were those of a child. To you everything was black or white, good or bad, you had. . . .'

'Not that much of a child!' she interrupted. 'Don't talk to me about Gisèle, it's in very bad taste. One does not discuss a man's first wife with his present one. I warn you, I'm not listening to what you say, so save your breath.'

It was with a definite sense of relief that she drew up in Serac, outside the butcher's shop, and deposited Bernard on the narrow pavement. He leant through the open door to thank her fulsomely again and again. She heard him vaguely and saw the twitch of a muslin curtain against the window of Tante Monique's house. If she had ever hoped to keep her solo trip to Rémy a secret that hope would be lying in ruins about her feet, but to be fair, she had never even thought of doing that.

When she had decided to go, she had done so in the certainty that when she returned there would be a battle, and having Bernard in the passenger seat, chattering about frozen meat and Gisèle, had given her no time to work out a defence. Then she was in the yard at La Barrière and the big Citroën was parked by the kitchen door.

Resolutely, she forced her face to its calm expression and collected her pile of parcels from the boot in an unhurried manner. She allowed herself a small sense of injustice. The Mini was *her* car, she had given it to herself for a twenty-second birthday present. That was three years ago. She had passed her test first time and there wasn't a bump or scratch on the little car's immaculate paintwork. That proved that she was a competent driver, didn't it? She had driven all the way here from London, further proof of her competence! She was twenty-five years old, well beyond the age when people could tell her what to do; she was a grown woman, not a child, and last but not least, she had called Jacques to come and check the car before she had driven it. That showed a sense of responsibility, didn't it?

These thoughts caused her back to snap straight and she marched into the house with a belligerent air about her. Yves was in the kitchen, turning from the range with a pot of fresh coffee in his hand and the cups and saucers were already on the table. Marianne flicked a glance at his face, there was a nasty gleam in his eyes and his mouth was a hard, straight line. She would pretend that there was nothing amiss and let him start the fighting!

'Good afternoon, Yves.' She kept the table between them as she deposited her packages. 'Did you have a good day in Brive?' She smiled pleasantly and checked her pile of parcels to ensure that she had not lost any.

'Madame.' It was an arrogantly courteous address, and the green sparks started to glow in her eyes. She was not going to sit quietly while he behaved like a teacher with a naughty pupil!

'I've had a splendid day,' she said brightly, 'and I've done all my shopping. Now everything's ready for Christmas. I'll have this lot,' she waved at her pile of packages, 'all in the post by tomorrow or the day after. Is that fresh coffee? It smells lovely. Pour me a cup, please, I'll just take off my coat.' She heard herself babbling and self-disgust shook her. She was behaving like a nervous teenager, like a child expecting punishment and trying to delay it. Defiantly, she raised her head.

'Let's get it over, shall we?' she said through her teeth as she struggled out of her coat and tossed it over the back of a chair.

'Get it over?' There was surprise in his voice.

'Yes.' She was managing to work herself into a fine temper. 'Get it over! You're angry because I took my car and went shopping in it when you said that I shouldn't. Well, let's have it in the open, shall we? If there's going to be a row, let's have it now. I don't think I did anything wrong.'

'Sit down and drink your coffee, Marianne, and lower

your voice. What I have to say can wait until later.' Yves's nostrils pinched with distaste. 'I do not quarrel with my wife while Sylvie is present. She goes home at five o'clock, until then I insist that you control yourself.'

'I'm in perfect control!' Marianne lowered her voice and spat the words at him. 'It's not me that's behaving like a sulky bear, and I refuse to wait until after five o'clock. If you've anything to say, say it now.' She left the safety of her table barricade and marched around to stand in front of him. 'Sitting there,' she hissed, 'looking superior. If you don't take that arrogant lord of creation look off your face, I'll slap it off!'

His hand shot out and caught her wrist, squeezing it painfully.

'You will not slap me, my dear wife. Try it and see where it gets you.' His fingers tightened on her arm and she choked back a whimper of pain. 'Since you insist upon it, we will have our little quarrel now, but you will not raise your voice, neither will you slap anyone.'

'I've a perfect right to drive *my* car anywhere I choose,' her eyes glittered green, 'and I will not be treated like a naughty child just because I've done something you don't approve of!' She tried to wriggle her arm free, and his fingers tightened painfully again and his other hand came to fasten on the heavy knot of hair in the nape of her neck, twisting it until the tears came to her eyes.

'Brute!' she gasped, biting her lip. 'A typical man! If you can't have your own way, you start demonstrating your physical superiority. I won't. . . .'

The words were cut off sharply as his mouth ground down on hers. His hand released her arm to swing around her, dragging her against him relentlessly, and his other hand, still twisted in her hair, held her head firmly. She heard herself moan and then came the sound of the kitchen door opening.

Sylvie surveyed her employers with rapture. Such

romance—her lips parted on a sigh of envy. If only Jacques . . .!

When Marianne was finally released, she felt herself incapable of movement. Her mouth was bruised, her eyes were swimming with tears and Sylvie had gone. She stumbled to a chair and sat down quickly.

'I suppose you think you've won!' She was defiant to the last. 'Well, you haven't. Brute force does not impress me.'

'It silences you,' Yves's eyes fastened on her swollen lip, 'and at that particular moment, that was all that mattered. Or do you care that Sylvie chatters like a monkey as soon as she gets home? I would have thought that you would have preferred all Serac not to know that I was—er—reprimanding you for driving when I had expressly forbidden it.' He raised his eyes to look at her keenly. 'Do you still wish to continue our quarrel, Marianne?'

'You don't quarrel,' her courage was returning, 'you simply try to cow me with violence.'

'I would be a fool to try to match words with you,' he smiled very slightly. 'You have a tongue like an asp, so what other means do I have but violent ones? I told you that you were not to drive and I meant it. The next time I shall put you across my knee, and it will be even more painful, that I promise you.'

Marianne looked down her nose at him and sniffed, a haughty sniff, and heard her husband chuckle. The insensitive brute was daring to laugh at her, and her temper started to rise again, but she crammed it down hastily. Yves had said that he wouldn't bandy words with her and her lip was throbbing and there would be purple marks on her arm, already she could see the red patches where his fingers had squeezed. She felt his hand on her shoulder.

'Shall we call a truce, *ma mie*? We have had our little quarrel and now there is no more to be said. I suggest we forget about it. You accused me of sulking, but I do not, so why should you? But you will remember for next time, yes?'

'I'd be happier if I knew why I mustn't drive,' she muttered. 'I don't mind not driving if I know why. It's the fact that you ordered me not to without giving any good reason that makes me mad. It's like waving a red rag at a bull.'

'It is winter,' he sighed with exasperation. 'The roads here can be very treacherous and you are not used to them. This is not a suburb of a city—if you had an accident, it might be hours before you were found. Is that a good enough reason, madame wife?'

Marianne lost his last words as she listened to the bumps and rattling coming from the pantry. 'What's that?' Her head came round with a jerk and she turned wide eyes on him. 'There's something in the pantry!' Her mind was suddenly filled with visions of vermin, squeaking and scuttling about her clean shelves, and she shuddered. 'Rats?' All the colour went from her face.

'It is only your Christmas present, Marianne. A little early, but I had to take him when he was ready. Go and see for yourself.' Yves pulled her out of her chair and forced her across to the pantry door, pushing it open with his foot. 'He seems to have made a little disorder, but it can soon be cleaned up.'

Marianne looked at the upturned basins on the floor, at the puddle of water and dog biscuits and then at the large brown and black puppy sat in the middle of the 'little disorder', and all thoughts of injustice, quarrels and brute force fled from her mind.

'He's beautiful!' She turned shining eyes on Yves. 'He's just the sort of dog I've always wanted, but you can't keep a dog in a flat in London, not when you're out working all day.' She grasped the puppy, laughing at his weight. 'How old is he, how big is he going to be?'

'He is four months old and he will be too big for you to

pick up, so don't start turning him into a lapdog.' Yves was brisk about it. 'He will not be much good as a guard dog yet, although he will probably growl at strangers once he becomes used to us, but he has a nasty, suspicious mind, which is one reason I choose him.'

Marianne buried her face in the pup's warm fur, then she looked up at her husband. 'Are you being crafty, Yves? I'm sure you haven't forgotten that neither Tante nor Bernard likes dogs. They'll possibly come here once more and then we shall never see them again. And that reminds me, I gave Bernard a lift into Rémy today. He had an appointment with Monsieur Matheus at the bank and his van wouldn't start. He was waiting for me when I'd finished my shopping and I had to give him a lift back as well.' She wrinkled her nose in distaste. 'He doesn't improve on acquaintance, though. When I was young, I thought he was a sneaky little pig, and now he's older I still think he's a sneaky pig, but he's clever with it now. He nearly had me convinced that I'm a narrow-minded old fuddy-duddy.'

'We will not speak of your drive today, if you please, Marianne. Each time I think of it I become angry. Sit there and make friends with your dog. You will have to exercise him every day and this I think will be good for you. You will have to take him out and so you will have less time for polishing and interior decorating.' Yves scowled at her. 'You seem to have had a paintbrush in your hand ever since we were married.' He grasped her shoulders and turned her to the light that fell from the kitchen window. A hard, rough hand touched her cheek briefly and a long finger traced the shadows underneath her eyes. 'You are too pale,' he said harshly, 'and you have been working too hard. Polishing, painting, making curtains, cooking—you should let Sylvie do more than she does.'

'What nonsense!' Marianne glared at him. 'I'm quite healthy and I'm as strong as a horse and you know it. I was never sick. Can you ever remember me being sick or ill when I lived here before? Hard work suits me,' she told him belligerently.

'It does not suit me to have you look pale and thin,' he said in a hard impersonal voice. 'Your dog's food is in the pantry, in a cardboard box. I brought enough to last him a month and he'll need three meals a day until he's six months old.' His face was amused as he looked at her seated in the dilapidated chair with the big pup on her lap. 'Don't spoil him,' was his parting remark as he went upstairs.

'He's getting quite human,' Marianne told the puppy. 'Not half as frozen as he was. Perhaps we can keep up the defrosting process between us.' She sat back in the chair and waited while the pup made himself comfortable on her knees. She found her eyelids dropping and decided that perhaps she was a bit tired. Her eyelids drooped some more and within less than a minute both she and the dog were fast asleep.

Marianne woke to a warm heaviness on her lap and the rattle of utensils. The pup grumbled sleepily as he felt himself disturbed and Marianne turned a jaundiced eye on Yves coming from the pantry with a crock of eggs in his hand. She yawned and asked muzzily, 'How long have I been asleep?'

'About half an hour.' He was selecting eggs and breaking them competently into a large basin. 'I thought we would have omelettes and cheese and then take the dog for a walk.'

With an air of surprise, she looked up at him. 'Are you coming as well?' She asked the question with wonder in her voice. 'Haven't you any work to do in the office? Isn't Bernard coming up with some more points for clarification?'

'Is that how it seems to you, Marianne? That I work all day and all evening as well?' He was looking at her closely. 'Are you getting bored?' The sardonic smile. 'Blame yourself, then. You can't say I didn't warn you how it would be, what it would be like.'

She watched him pour oil in the pan and begin to beat eggs vigorously while the oil heated, all the while chiding herself for making a remark which had brought the hard, dark suspicion back to his face. Then she shook herself fully awake. Why should she feel guilty about a chance remark, a perfectly innocent remark? She let herself relax back in the chair, playing with the pup's stiff ears while Yves poured the beaten eggs into the hot pan. With his back to her, his voice came muffled. 'And don't let that dog get ideas about sleeping with you. There is no room in the bed for him. I expect he will be crying for company tonight, but let him cry. He'll soon get used to sleeping on his own.' Expertly he turned out the big, fluffy omelette on to a hot plate and cut it in half, putting one portion on to another plate which he had been warming in the oven.

'You can make omelettes any time you like.' Marianne wiped the last traces from her plate with a piece of bread. 'That was good!'

'Are you bored?' Yves's grey eyes watched her closely while his face remained enigmatic. 'I said you would be.'

Marianne suspected a note of satisfaction in his deep voice, as if he was pleased that his prophecy had been correct. She glared at him. 'I'm not bored,' she poured herself another cup of coffee. 'Sometimes I get a little lonely, but that's not the same as being bored. It just means that I haven't anyone to talk to. Sylvie's a nice girl and she keeps me up to date with what's going on in the village, but you couldn't call her a brilliant conversationalist, could you? That means that I haven't anybody to discuss things with.'

'I am always willing to discuss things with you.'

'Only when you have time,' she snorted. 'When are you ever here to discuss things with me? You've usually left the house by the time I get up, you work all day, you hardly speak when you do come in and since Bernard has started on about this deep freeze business, I see even less of you.' She was getting into her stride. 'It was bad enough before, when you shut yourself in the office every evening. You do it deliberately because there's no real reason why you should spend every evening in the office, not unless you really want to.'

'You think I do it to annoy you?' The sardonic note was back in his voice. 'You flatter yourself, madame wife.'

'I'm not flattering myself, or you either for that matter,' she retorted swiftly. 'You're always talking about how practical you are, but you're not very practical at all or you wouldn't spend all those hours on paper work as you do. Get me a typewriter and I could do seventy-five per cent of your evening work in one hour. But then, of course,' she allowed herself a small smile, 'you wouldn't have anywhere to hide in the evening, would you?'

'I do not hide!'

'Yes, you do.' She was serene. 'You hide yourself during the day, either somewhere on the farm or else down in the vineyard, and then come home, have a meal and hide some more in the office until it's time to go to bed. What are you afraid of, Yves? Is it me or is it just that you find me repulsive except in the dark? Could it be that your taste runs to well-built women, is that why you complain that I'm thin? Or is there some other reason why you hide?'

'I do *not* hide,' he repeated the denial with a rasp of irritation. 'And if I did, who would not in my position, married to you, Madame Mosquito? You fly in from all directions and sting with your sharp little tongue. What peace is there for a man with such a wife?' He shrugged himself into his jacket and tossed hers across to her. 'Come along, the dog needs exercise, so put your boots on. Don't teeter around in those stupid high heels or you'll break an ankle in the dark.'

'How charming you can be when you try,' she mocked

as she struggled with the long zips of her high boots. 'Many women wouldn't put up with it. I don't know that I will for much longer. Liz asked me to join her in Switzerland for Christmas and I'm tempted to take her up on the offer.' From under her lashes, she watched his face. Would there be any reaction to her brave words? she wondered. Perhaps it was too soon to be fighting back. Maybe she should have waited a little longer, left it until the New Year. If she had hoped for a reaction, she was disappointed. Yves's face remained a mocking mask.

'Did I not say that you were bored?'

'I'm not bored,' she answered him waspishly. 'You are intolerable.' With a small sigh of defeat she put on her coat. He was not only intolerable, he was infuriating as well, taking her own words and turning them against her, proving his point with her own denial of it. It was almost as though he wanted her to be bored, wanted her to go off in a huff and leave him. 'Bitter little misogynist, aren't you?' she offered as he held the door open for her. Temper was flaring in her and she wanted to shake him until his teeth rattled, and the absolute physical impossibility of her ever being able to do so made her quite pink with frustration.

'A misogynist? Is that what you think of me? It would be rude of me to contradict you, Marianne,' Yves said nastily as he took her arm, leading her out of the yard and on to the narrow road. The puppy strained at his lead, he was a big, strong pup and Marianne's arm, the one that held the lead, felt as if it was being pulled out of its socket. 'Permit me,' Yves spoke quietly in the darkness and she could have sworn that there was amusement in his voice. His warm hand covered hers, taking the lead from her fingers. 'It is essential to be firm when training a German Shepherd which will be as big as this one.'

They walked on companionably in the crisp night air, the darkness enclosing them like a blanket. Marianne looked back over her shoulder, but a bend in the road hid the light which she had left burning in the kitchen. Over to her left and what seemed like a long way below her in the narrow rounded valley, a few lights twinkled from Serac Ste. Marie. It was pleasant walking like this in the dark and she felt herself relaxing. Since it was dark, she had no need to school her features not to betray her thoughts. She felt quite safe to allow her usual cool smile to develop into a Cheshire Cat grin, if she felt like it!

About two hours later, an unaccustomed noise broke her free of the light sleep into which she had fallen. Wide awake now, she lay in the darkness waiting for the noise to repeat itself. It came again, a mournful whine that quavered to end in a high note. The pup! She wondered what he was doing. Quietly she started to slide out of bed, mentally visualising the position of her slippers and dressing gown, but her slide was stopped by a strong hard arm that came swiftly about her.

'No. . . .' Yves's voice was slurred with sleep. 'Leave him, he will soon become used to being on his own.' Another mournful howl came from the kitchen.

'There, listen to him!' She tried to struggle free of the encompassing arm. 'I must go down, Yves. I can't just lie here and listen to him crying like that.' There was no relaxing of the arm about her, if anything it tightened, pulling her closer to his side. More lonely little howls and whines rose in a crescendo of misery and Marianne redoubled her efforts to get out of bed with a conspicuous lack of success. 'I *must* go!' She was desperate. 'Perhaps he's ill, perhaps the food you brought doesn't agree with him. He might have hurt himself. . . .'

'Marianne,' Yves yawned, 'one thing about you has not changed since you went away. You still talk too much, but I can stop that, I think.' His weight came upon her and his mouth stifled her gasp of outrage. For a very short while she struggled against him ineffectually before yielding to the insidious caress of his hands and mouth.

'You're a monster,' she sighed the words against his mouth. 'You have no pity. That poor little dog!'

'What poor little dog?' he enquired reasonably.

Marianne listened. Not a sound broke the quiet stillness of the night in the old farmhouse. Reluctantly she chuckled. 'He's gone to sleep, you were right after all!'

'You admit it? That this intolerable, pitiless monster could possibly know better than you?' There was the ghost of a laugh from the recumbent figure in the bed beside her. 'Emulate your dog, Marianne, and go to sleep too. Tomorrow, I will buy you a typewriter.'

CHAPTER SIX

THE New Year came in with a brisk flurry of snow falling from leaden skies. The road down to Serac Ste. Marie was impassable to vehicles, the fallen snow lying upon a layer of ice. In the sharp bends of the hill, the wind had blown it so that it piled up, smooth and deceptive, giving no hint of the treacherous curves beneath the surface. Marianne peered through the kitchen window and then turned her back on the grey and white landscape where the black skeletons of trees stood stark against the pale background. Fiercely she confronted her husband.

'If you'd bought that Land Rover when I wanted you to, you wouldn't have been unable to get down to the vineyard.' There was a bite in her voice. 'These last few days have been like living with a caged tiger,' she informed him, her eyes sparkling green with irritation. 'You're prowling in and out and you always leave the doors open, so that the kitchen gets cold. We might as well be living in a refrigerator!'

Marianne was warmly dressed in slacks with a thick, soft

polo-necked jumper, and her hair was tied back rather haphazardly with a piece of ribbon. She shivered in spite of her warm clothing and returned to the attack, 'Grand'mère would have. . . .'

'Grand'mère is dead,' Yves interrupted her in a flat voice. 'She has been dead ever since last September. Must you be forever resurrecting her?' He caught Marianne's look of shock and his face became grim. 'Grand'mère is no longer part of La Barrière, but you still drag her out whenever something is not to your liking.'

'Yves!' She turned disbelieving eyes on him. 'You make it sound as though you hated her, and you didn't, I know that.'

Sardonically, he returned her look. 'To you, Marianne, Grand'mère was everything that was perfect, no? And during the years you spent in England, you fed on your memories, discarding the not so happy ones and building up a picture of a woman who did not exist. An all-knowing, all-wise woman, an earth mother goddess, as remote from the real woman as the North Pole is from the South.' He laughed briefly; it had a bitter, unhappy sound as though he looked back on a deep hurt. 'You should have been here during those years.' His mouth twisted, mocking her. 'You would have seen things very differently.'

Marianne shook her head. 'I don't believe you. Grand'mère was. . . .'

'Grand'mère was?' He drew on his pipe and then regarded her through the haze of blue smoke. 'I'll tell you what Grand'mère was, since you don't seem to remember. Grand'mère was always right, wasn't she? And she trained you well, didn't she? Do you know what you were in the old days? You were a little pale echo of the old woman. You agreed with her on everything. You even agreed with her when she arranged my marriage to Gisèle, didn't you? You knew what Gisèle was, but you went to Grand'mère's side, remember? You stood by the window in the salon and you went to comfort *her*!' His hands were hard on her arms, she could feel the pressure of his fingers through the soft wool, gripping, bruising. 'You knew,' he reiterated, and Marianne nodded slightly, whereupon he shook her. 'But you didn't even say a word, you went to Grand'mère's side and you both stood silent and condemned me, both of you, without allowing me to say a word in defence. I looked at your faces and it was all there. I was twenty-five years old, a man, not a boy, but you condemned me. You gave me no chance, either of you.'

The torrent of words was making Marianne breathless. To think that all this hurt, all this bitterness should have been festering inside him for all these years—but he hadn't finished. He placed his hand on her chest and pushed her down in the chair and stood over her, his eyes blazing and his face nearly as white as her own.

'Grand'mère and you,' his hands were clenched on the arms of the chair, she could not escape this bitter torrent that poured over her. 'You were my judges and my jury, and because I loved La Barrière, I had to accept her verdict if I wanted to stay here. Those few years after you went to England, I lived in hell! She and Gisèle kept up a constant war, each one aggravating the other until the house became a battleground, and they expected me to live in it! Live in it with two cats fighting every day and all day. Gisèle whining to me that she had expected to be mistress in her new home, then Grand'mère telling me what I should do.' Yves laughed grimly down at Marianne's colourless face. 'Telling me to take Gisèle to my bed and beget children! Make the best of a bad bargain! And then, after Gisèle was killed, what did the old witch do but arrange another marriage for me, only this time it was you.'

Marianne cowered back in the chair, her heart aching with pity and tears making a painful knot in her throat. 'You mean. . . .' Then she caught herself up, her voice was shaking and she made an effort to control it. 'But you didn't have to marry me, did you? That ridiculous will could have been set aside, and you knew that. Any competent lawyer could have done it for you.'

'So! You knew that too?' His voice was soft and dangerous. 'That puts an entirely different complexion on the affair.'

'I can't see how it alters anything,' the pity and regret had been driven from her mind and she was beginning to feel definitely ill used. 'You had no need to marry me at all, so why did you?'

'Perhaps to punish you.' His face was once more an expressionless mask.

'Punish me? What for?' She looked up at him as if she had never seen him before.

'For four years of hell on earth, madame wife. What else? A few words from you and Grand'mère would have taken time to think, even if she would not change her mind. But you, you didn't say those few words, did you? No! You stood at her side supporting her, your little white virgin's face full of horror that a man should behave like a man and not like one of the plaster saints down in the church.' He jerked his head to indicate Serac. 'Four years of wedded bliss!' his laughter came grim and mocking, 'and when they were over, four more years of suspicion that I would once more give way to my disgusting male instincts. Do you think I cared what they said in Serac? But what she thought, that was important. She watched my every move. I could not even speak to a woman without she accused me of anything and everything her twisted mind could dream up. Grand'mère had a lot to answer for.'

'So you married me to punish me, did you?' With an effort, Marianne kept the horror out of her voice and raised her eyes to his, her own face a smooth cool mask that showed nothing of her inner turmoil or of the painful pity that still filled her. Only the whitened knuckles of her hands on the arms of the chair gave any clue to the state of her mind. 'And how long do you intend this punishment to last—one year, two years, four? I don't have to stay here, you know. I could walk out tomorrow. I'm financially independent and I'm a good secretary, I can always get another job.'

'Oh no, Marianne,' his grey eyes glittered at her, 'you do not escape as easily as that. You like some parts of being married, you like them very much. You will stay if only because you've developed a taste for being married. I think you were born a Puritan, despite your almost wanton behaviour at times, and Grand'mère did her work well on you. You could not go to another man while you are married to me, could you? Your conscience wouldn't let you. So you see, you suffer more than Gisèle. She had no such inhibitions. Any man would do for her.'

Marianne laughed at him with what she hoped sounded like soft amusement. 'Yves!' she shook her head at him. 'You're a fraud, you like being married too. As I said before, you didn't *have* to marry me. Nobody forced you into it. You didn't do it to please Grand'mère and you didn't do it to please me, so you must have done it to please yourself! As for punishing me. . . .' she chuckled, 'you don't seem to be having much success in that direction, perhaps you'd better try harder.'

'Almost you tempt me, madame wife.' It was barely a whisper, a threat lying not far below the surface, and the heavy lids had fallen over his eyes so that they gleamed like steely slits in his tanned face.

'Then I'll leave you to think up something truly diabolical.' Marianne pushed him away and rose from the chair. 'Simply because you can't work, it doesn't mean that I can't find anything to do. I'm going up to Grand'mère's room and I'm going to turn out her drawers and empty her wardrobe. Anything good I'm sending down to Sylvie's mother, the rest I shall burn.'

'Burn everything.' The deep voice floated up the stairs after her.

Half way up the stairs, her common sense reasserted itself. Yves had been cooped up in the house for several days, unable to go farther than the barn, and for an active man, that must be torture. No wonder he had become irritable and started feeling sorry for himself. But that was no excuse for thinking nasty things about Grand'mère! As for his 'burn everything'—no, she couldn't do that. It would be like sacrilege, and while she was only too pleased to exorcise Gisèle's ghost from the salon, she wanted to keep at least some part of Grand'mère. Grand'mère was a warm, cosy ghost. Despite anything Yves said, Grand'mère had made this house a home for her, she had taught her everything she knew about life. Marianne stopped here, remembering her abysmal ignorance when she had first arrived in London. She banished the thought almost before it had formed. Grand'mère had cared for her, loved her, and she determined to remember that. But once in the big white bedroom, she found nothing of this. The bedroom, the biggest in the house, was bleak and spartan. Could Yves have been right? She dismissed the thought and returned to childhood memories.

When she thought of Grand'mère, it was always in the kitchen, her back poker-straight in the black which she always wore, and yet—Marianne hesitated; this was Grand'mère's room, surely there would be something of that here? She glanced around. Everything was in order; Sylvie cleaned and dusted every week, but Sylvie was not the author of this immaculate tidiness. It was just a place to sleep. There was not even one comfortable chair or a rug in the room, there was not one touch to soften the chill austerity. Marianne wandered over to the big chest of drawers, not even a mirror. Had Grand'mère been like that underneath, prim and austere?

Marianne tried to recall more of her childhood. It had been good growing up at La Barrière, it was a lovely safe place for a child to live. Grand'mère's rules were rigid; everything was either good or bad, there were no grey areas, everything was a clear black or white. To tell fibs or to be disobedient was bad, to go to school and to work hard was good, so one knew how one must behave. To be clean and neat was good, to obey was good, she remembered Grand'mère saying so! Good children obeyed their elders, it was written in the Commandments, and she had been a good child. There had been lapses, of course—her lips curved into a nostalgic smile—like the time she had fallen into the river, but it had been a hot day and Yves had pulled her out. She remembered Grand'mère's tart rebuke to Yves for letting her fall in the river and the scolding he had received when she had fallen in the duckpond.

Always Yves had received the scoldings because she, Marianne, was a good girl and none of these dreadful things would have happened to her if she hadn't been led astray. Marianne sighed and decided that she must have been a priggish little horror.

With an idle hand she opened the wardrobe. Grand'mère's clothes, dresses and skirts all hung there primly, all in unrelieved black, and at the bottom, two pairs of boots and one of shoes stood, ready polished for their next wearing. Marianne had not remembered that the old lady always wore boots except on very grand occasions.

She opened a drawer in the massive chest. Underwear. Plain white cotton, not a frill, not a scrap of lace nor a bit of ribbon anywhere. Marianne sighed; this was a side to Grand'mère which she had never considered, an austere, rigidly uncompromising side, totally unlike the woman of her memory. Up here was Yves's martinet, her remem-berances were downstairs in the kitchen, but they were the same woman. How could two people have such widely different memories of the same person? Could it be that the truth lay somewhere between the two opposing points of view?

Quietly she left the bedroom, closing the door behind her. Sylvie could clear the room, to her the chill formality would mean nothing. She would giggle at the boots and the old-fashioned clothing and cheerfully carry it all out to be burned. Marianne hurried to the kitchen; the chill of the bedroom had gone right through to her bones.

Yves had made fresh coffee and she accepted a cup gratefully, holding it so that it warmed her fingers. He looked at her mockingly.

'And have you decided what you will keep, what you will throw away? It was not a hard task, was it?'

Marianne refused to look at him, but wandered across to the window and stood looking out at the snowy landscape. 'Sylvie can see to it,' and then grudgingly, 'as you said, we'll burn everything.'

'Then that leaves us two things to do, one can be done any time but for the other, we will have to wait until the roads are passable.' Yves came across to stand behind her. 'I am sorry if I have forced you to see a side of Grand'mère that you had never thought of before.'

Marianne ignored this last remark and concentrated on the two things he had said they had to do. That was merely 'things to do', the other made her feel sick inside. 'What do we have to do?' She made her voice level and calm.

'First of all, we should give your dog a name, don't you think? You cannot keep calling him "pup".'

Marianne was glad of such a mundane subject. Anything to keep her mind off her memories. 'I thought of Dominic, but then I went off it. It's difficult to shorten and you can't go round shouting "Dominic!", can you?' She was babbling again, she could hear her voice becoming shrill. With a muttered excuse she pushed past him and ran upstairs to the little room she had used as a child. She heard Yves follow her and she went to the window, turning her back on him.

'Go away,' she said between her teeth, then jumped as his hand came upon her shoulder.

'Come and wash your face.' It was a command, but Marianne was not feeling like being commanded. She tried to shake her shoulder free.

'Leave me alone!' The words were half muttered under her breath.

'All this fuss because I tried to make you see that people aren't always what you think they are. It's no use you worshipping a fictional person, you've got to take the good and bad together. Everybody's part good and part bad, and Grand'mère was no exception.'

'You won't leave me anything, will you? You want to bring everyone down to your level. I've got to see them as you see them or I'm wrong.' Marianne pushed a hand through her hair. 'I loved Grand'mère, and it doesn't matter what you say, I'll go on loving her.'

'Have I asked you not to? If you loved the old lady, she must have earned that love.'

'And what did she earn from you?' Marianne almost whispered the question.

'Respect. She had her standards and she kept to them.'

'Only respect?'

'How could there have been more? I also have my standards, but they were never the same as hers, and that she didn't understand. Now come and wash your face, there have been enough histrionics for one day and lunch will be ready soon, I hope.'

'A name for your dog.' Yves poured hot coffee and added cream and sugar before passing it to Marianne.

'Ludovic—and what are you doing putting cream and sugar in my coffee? I don't like it like that.' Marianne was still a bit snappish, she felt brittle.

'It's as good a name as any. I suppose it will get

shortened to Ludo—and you are having cream and sugar because I think you are getting too thin.' Yves didn't raise his head, so she had no idea what his expression was. His voice sounded unconcerned.

Marianne sighed with exasperation. 'I thought we'd gone into that already. I'm no thinner now than when I came at the end of September. I like myself the way I am.' A thought occurred to her. 'You said there were two things, one was to name the dog and we've done that. What was the other?'

His face was wearing its usual mask of non-expression when he raised his head. 'In November I ordered a Land Rover. I had a telephone call from the garage in Clermont this morning, to say the vehicle has been delivered. I told them that we would pick it up as soon as the roads were passable.'

'You ordered a Land Rover?'

'Yes, *ma mie*—you talked me into it, don't you remember? It was to be so useful, a serviceable vehicle, one we needed on these roads in the winter. You even mentioned that I could tow things about.' What could very well have passed for a smile curved his mouth slightly.

'And my Mini? What are we going to do about that?' Marianne felt a small excitement creeping through her. 'Do they have part exchange in France? Because if they don't, I believe Jacques would like to buy it—he looks at it with envy and he told me that if it was properly tuned, it would do many more kilometres to the hour. We could put it in the garage at Clermont and have it overhauled, we'd have to go there in it, and then when it was ready, you could come to some arrangement with Jacques about paying for it. Sylvie told me they have some small savings, but I wouldn't like them to have to spend all their money on a car, they must be saving up to get married.'

'You go too fast once more, madame wife. As you say, Jacques would very much like to buy the Mini, but it is your car, you must put a price on it and the money will be paid to you.'

'I thought we were partners, sort of. I don't want any "yours" and "mine". Besides, how do I know what a Mini is worth in France? It won't be very much because it's classed as a foreign car and sometimes it's difficult to get spares. . . .'

Yves sighed, 'Why do you always make difficulties, Marianne? A small matter, the sale of your car, and already it has assumed gigantic proportions!'

'You see to it, then.' Marianne kept a straight face, although she was laughing inside herself. 'But don't charge Jacques too much, if he and Sylvie are getting married they'll need all the money they can get. There'll be furniture to buy and they'll have to find somewhere to live. . . .'

'Another problem?' Yves sounded disgusted and Marianne began to enjoy herself. Problems seemed to be Yves's strong point, they seemed to take his mind off his grievances. Well, that was all to the good, she could make problems ad infinitum. The simplest thing could be magnified out of all proportion; all she had to do was to worry aloud.

During the third week in January it started to rain, and while this made taking Ludo for his exercise an uncomfortable affair and filled the porch up with wet raincoats and wellingtons, at least it made the hill down to Serac passable and they could go and fetch the Land Rover and, as arranged, leave the Mini for an overhaul, after which Jacques was going to buy it. Marianne smiled as she remembered that Sylvie had worked for a whole week with an unasked question trembling on her lips before Jacques finally agreed on a price with Yves. Sylvie's eyes had been big and round and full of questions.

The Mini ploughed along the wet roads, flinging mud and spray all over itself, and Yves laughed at the size of the gearstick and the way he had to fold himself up to get into the seat behind the steering wheel. Marianne didn't mind how much he laughed at her car or at anything, herself included. When she had first come back to La Barrière, he had never laughed; now he seemed to have thawed out a bit, but experience had shown that she must not allow herself to be carried away by one humorous moment.

They left the Mini in the garage at Clermont. Jacques was to pick it up later, and Marianne started to see difficulties ahead. She worried all through lunch about export and import. After all, she had, however unknowingly, exported a car from England and imported it into France, and now she was going to sell it. Some Customs official was going to come waving forms at her, of that she was sure. At last she mentioned it to Yves, who raised his eyebrows in astonishment.

'Why should they come to you?'

'It's my car,' she pointed out, her mouth drooping with gloomy thoughts.

'But you are my wife and this is France,' he mocked her puzzlement. 'Any business with the Customs will, as a matter of course, come to me. Poor Marianne,' his eyes sparkled with some emotion and she could not tell what it was, meanwhile he jeered at her. 'Have you forgotten? You've gone back to being a chattel again. No more Women's Lib. Are you going to burn your bra in defiance of me?' His gaze lingered on her quite charming bosom before coming back to her face. It was an intimate look and she felt herself go pink with embarrassment. This brought a nasty smile to his face, a sardonic smile, she decided.

'My underwear and what I do with it are none of your business—and I don't care to discuss the subject in a restaurant,' she hissed at him.

Halfway home in the Land Rover, she began to regret the disposal of her Mini. In her opinion, the springing of the Land Rover left a lot to be desired and, worse than this, the vehicle seemed to be full of draughts. She shivered inside her sheepskin coat and looked warily at the controls. They looked very complicated, although Yves seemed to be perfectly at home with them. If ever Yves raised his ban on her driving, she would never be able to manage this vehicle, so that ended any possibility of her making solo trips to Rémy. Back to square one!

Almost at once she decided that even if she had to accept Yves as a chauffeur, she did not want to be driven around in a Land Rover. It was a spartan vehicle, the Citroën would be much nicer. She thought of the Citroën's lovely suspension that ironed out bumps and uneven bits of road, the comfort of the seating and the very efficient heater. She would have to twist Yves's arm a bit, and she spent the rest of the journey home in thoughtful silence.

In her bedroom at half past six, Marianne stepped back from the mirror and examined herself as well as she could. She was *not* thin—she twisted herself to look from another angle—she was slender, a much nicer word even if it did mean the same thing.

She had just treated herself to a leisurely soak in a bath which smelled nicely of gardenia and she was going to array herself in an old black dress that was cut to emphasise her slender waist and was also short enough to allow her to wear flat sandals which would knock at least two inches from her height.

She wanted to appear small and fragile, so fragile that bouncing around in a hard-sprung Land Rover would possibly cause her to wilt away if she didn't snap in half first. The black dress lay ready on the bed, the dinner was cooking nicely and Sylvie had lit fires in both the salon and the dining room, so Marianne had plenty of time to do things with her face.

A little eyeshadow to emphasise her eyes, she thought; a very little rouge high on her cheekbones to give her eyes a false sparkle, a pretty and delicate browny pink lipstick, all this together with a pale cream foundation would increase the fragile impression given by the black dress.

She noted with some pleasure that the wide wedding ring plus the equally wide engagement ring with its heavy setting for the big emerald made her hand appear too thin and weak to support the weight of them, and she hunted out a piece of narrow black ribbon and pinned an old cameo to it. Tied around her throat, it would enhance her pale skin and make her neck look like a stalk.

She did her face and slipped into the black dress. After hunting out a pair of flat sandals and cramming her feet into them, she stood back from the mirror and admired the result. Except for the brushing of rouge on her cheekbones, she looked bloodless and practically on the point of death.

Yves entered the bedroom just as she was tying the black velvet ribbon about her neck. She caught a faint whiff of aftershave and swiftly concealed a grin. Yves had abandoned the carbolic soap!

'Tante Monique and Bernard have invited themselves for dinner,' he began, then, '*Ciel*! What have you done with yourself?' His hands found her shoulders, turning her to face him while his eyes roved over her. 'Are you ill?' he demanded peremptorily.

Marianne straightened her back and raised her chin, thereby managing to look weakly defiant. 'Of course I'm not ill. I'm never ill, you know that!'

'Tante and Bernard will think I'm starving you.' His hands slid to her waist. 'You appear to be thinner than ever, much thinner than when you arrived at the end of September.' Suddenly his eyes gleamed. 'You've done this deliberately, haven't you, Marianne? And for my benefit, I suppose, since you did not know that we would have visitors.' He pulled her close to him and studied her face with great intensity. 'A pity we have visitors,' he murmured, and Marianne flushed and pulled away from him. The look in his eyes was warm and inviting and Marianne found herself regretting Tante and Bernard's presence downstairs.

'At any rate,' Yves's mouth twisted in its usual sardonic lines as she released herself, 'I've managed to bring a little real colour to your face.'

She wriggled free of his hands. 'I'd better go down straight away. The table is only laid for two.' She felt rather cross; all her work had been in vain. She looked up at him from her reduced height and gave him a pathetic smile which was rather spoiled by the rage which glittered in her eyes. With a snort of disgust, she flounced from the room and halfway down the stairs, the import of what Yves had said hit her and she had to restrain herself from rushing back upstairs to change.

Damn Tante Monique and Bernard! She ground her excellent white teeth. This would mean another evening spent with Yves's aunt, sitting in the salon with not a thing to say except to agree with each and every one of Tante's rigid dictums, while Yves and Bernard discussed business in the office. It wasn't going to be like that, she decided grimly, not tonight and not if she could help it! Whatever business was going on, they could damn well discuss it in the salon, in front of her, and she would sit at the table and take shorthand notes!

Without bothering to go into the salon and make her visitors welcome, she went directly to the kitchen, put two more plates to warm and then bustled into the dining room to lay up another two places. At the same time, she put away the candelabra, two very nice silver ones with which she had adorned the table. There was no sense in wasting soft lights on Tante Monique! Then she went back to the kitchen to cover her dress with her large white apron while she made a sauce from the fragrant stock that was bubbling softly around the boned and rolled ribs of beef. She spared a glance for her caramel creams and was glad she had decided to keep the remainder of the apples for another occasion. Tante liked caramel creams and the apples which were stored in the barn were dwindling rapidly. Another few tarts and they would all be gone.

With only half her mind on what she was doing, she started to ladle soup into the tureen, and it was while she was doing this that Yves came into the kitchen. He looked suave and well dressed in black pants and a matching shirt, the sombreness relieved by a red silk cravat which he had tied about his throat, the ends tucked into the open collar of his shirt. He moved around the table to come behind her. 'Shall I carry this tureen in for you, *ma mie*?' he murmured. 'You look frail enough to drop it.' Marianne gritted her teeth and flashed him a look of intense dislike.

'Carry it if you wish,' she kept her voice low and spoke over her shoulder, 'and you can carve the meat, if you like.' She gasped as he deliberately bent his head and bit her earlobe.

'Perhaps it would be better,' the smile that curved his mouth was wicked. 'It is, if I remember, a very sharp knife, and you look at me as if you would like to cut my throat.'

Suddenly Marianne giggled at the ridiculous situation. All her care, the wearing of this black dress that made her look like a beanpole, it had all been wasted. Yves had seen through it after only a few seconds.

'Never mind!' he consoled as if she had spoken her thoughts aloud. 'Only one look at you and both Tante and Bernard will be convinced that I am ill-treating you. What you need to be really convincing is a bruise or two.' She felt his mouth warm on the skin of her neck and whirled herself away with a breathless laugh. This was a new Yves and she needed time to adjust.

It was after half past eleven when at last their uninvited guests departed and as Yves closed the door behind them, Marianne went carefully back to the salon and collapsed on to the gold velvet of the couch laughing hysterically.

'Did you *see* them?' she gasped. 'Tante Monique is convinced that I'm consumptive and Bernard. . . .' She looked up to see Yves regarding her thoughtfully.

'So,' he said dryly, 'the little Marianne is not dead, not quite. You can still laugh—I thought you had forgotten how.'

'You've given me precious little to laugh at since I've been here.' Marianne was pot-valiant having drunk two sherries, three large glasses of wine and had a cognac with her coffee. 'You've behaved very boorishly,' she informed him, 'ever since I came back. Boorish, arrogant and uncommunicative.' Her tongue stumbled over the last word and she giggled again. 'As for my laughter, it's probably the result of wine and cognac. I'll be back to normal tomorrow.' A faint mournful howl interrupted her. 'That's Ludo,' she nodded gravely. 'I put him in the pantry when I knew we had visitors and he's been there all evening. He's been uncomfortable.' She found herself speaking very slowly and carefully, enunciating each word precisely because otherwise they ran into each other. 'Let him out, please.'

'And you, Marianne, are a little drunk, I think. Go up to bed, I will attend to the dog. Can you manage the stairs by yourself?'

With enormous dignity she rose to her feet. 'Insulting man!' she said firmly, and walked past him and through the door with immense care and precision. Halfway up the stairs, her care and precision vanished and she sat down abruptly. It was there that her husband found her, her head leaned against the banister rail.

'Tut-tut! Not only a nagging wife but a drunken one as well!' He lifted her easily and carried her up to the bedroom, where he dumped her unceremoniously on the bed and rolled her over to unzip her dress. Like a doll, she allowed herself to be undressed and then fell back unprotestingly on to her pillow, her eyes closed and a seraphic smile on her face. Yves was now wearing his brooding look and she opened her eyes and wagged an admonitory finger at him. 'You should smile more often,' she admonished, slurring the words, and closed her eyes again so that she did not see his wry smile nor did she hear his, 'No more than two glasses of wine in future, and *no* cognac, Marianne!'

Sylvie woke her in the morning and Marianne opened dull eyes and raised a hand to her aching head. She could remember climbing the stairs, but after that, nothing! A flush of shame swamped her whole body and she accepted a cup of coffee with an unsteady hand.

'Monsieur Bernard Fortin is waiting to speak to you, *madame*,' Sylvie smiled, and Marianne closed her eyes to shut out the sight of so much health and vigour. 'I wished him to wait in the salon, but he would not. He sits in the kitchen.'

'Bernard here?' Marianne clutched the covers about her. Yves had undressed her but he had not bothered to go any further; her nightgown lay in undisturbed folds across the chair by the bed. 'Whatever time is it?'

'It is ten o'clock, *madame*. I came as usual at seven,' Sylvie was virtuous, 'but Monsieur Yves said that I must wait and leave you to sleep this morning. I have put the dog out in the yard, *madame*. Monsieur Fortin seems not to like dogs and the little one growled at him. He is a fine puppy, is he not? Jacques, who brought me this morning, says that he will be very large.' Sylvie chattered on happily, moving about the room, collecting Marianne's soiled clothing and the shirt which Yves had worn the previous evening.

'All right, Sylvie, tell Monsieur Bernard that I will be with him in fifteen minutes—and make some fresh coffee, please.' As Sylvie vanished, her arms full of washing, Marianne made a mad dash for the bathroom, shivering as the cold air touched her skin. She used five of her fifteen minutes under the shower and emerged, wrapped in a towel to scrabble through drawers for clean underwear and to hunt through the wardrobe for a pair of dark green slacks. She topped these with a matching polo-necked sweater, pushed her feet into sandals and dragged a brush through her hair to tie it back with a piece of ribbon. She lamented, as she always did, that her hair was not a definite dark red, she would have much preferred that to its pale marmalade colour. After adding a touch of lipstick, she called into the bathroom on her way downstairs to the kitchen. She wanted—no, that was the wrong word, she needed aspirin and there was a bottle of them in the bathroom cabinet. Whatever it was that Bernard wanted would have to wait until she had drunk a cup of coffee and taken her two aspirin. She vowed, holding her hand to her cold, clammy forehead, that never again would she so much as look at the cognac bottle.

Bernard rose to his feet as she went into the kitchen. His flat, unemotional eyes slid over her appreciatively while his plump face registered concern.

'Marianne. . . .' he began, but she waved him aside to go and fetch cups and saucers from the dresser and poured hot coffee into them. The aspirin, which she had slipped into the pocket of her slacks, she retrieved and surreptitiously swallowed them with her coffee.

'Marianne——' Bernard began again, ignoring the coffee which she had set before him, then he gasped, 'Marianne, you are not taking *drugs*!' His voice rose in horror.

She raised a surprised face at him from the contemplation of her coffee cup. 'Drugs? What on earth are you talking about?'

'You must seek medical attention at once,' he babbled. 'Before the filthy stuff gets a hold on you. Oh, to think that it should have come to this! That you should seek relief from that brute by taking drugs!' His features were contorted into an expression compounded of horror, pity and misery. Marianne laughed in his face.

'I've just taken two aspirins,' she told him tartly. 'The only thing I seek relief from is a headache brought on by drinking too much wine last night and following it up with a glass of cognac.'

The pity, the misery and the horror did not leave his face, they were joined by sadness. 'It is as I thought, then. You seek oblivion in alcohol. I said as much to Maman last night when we arrived home. We both remarked how frail you had become. Leave him, Marianne, before it is too late, before the craving takes a firm hold on you. You can go back to England, start a new life. I will help you to escape.' His hand reached across the table to cover hers. 'You will need help, now that he has sold your car. I will drive you to Clermont and from there you can take a train to Paris.'

Marianne listened, so stupefied by rage that she was unable to speak for several seconds. Then as the full meaning of his words hit her, she dragged her hand from under his.

'Get out!' she hissed at him. 'Get out and don't ever let me see your revolting face here again. You—you vilifier! How dare you say such things!' She rose from her chair and came around the table to him, anger making her hands strong to drag him from the chair and push him across to the door. '*Out*!' she ordered, rage giving her voice a shrill note.

Bernard, protesting, found himself thrust outside and turned back to speak, but Ludo, who had run to join Marianne on the step, growled warningly. Bernard was faced with a white-faced virago and a young dog who was uneasy and showing an alarming number of large teeth. Discretion overcame him and he sidled crabwise to the door of his van, opened it and with ludicrous speed got in and drove off. Marianne went back to the kitchen and sat down quickly, her legs trembling so much she was afraid to stand.

'Sylvie!' she called, and when the girl appeared, Marianne motioned her with a trembling hand to fetch another cup and the coffee pot and to sit down.

'You were listening at the door.' It was not a question, Marianne put it as a statement of fact and Sylvie nodded. 'You are not to admit Monsieur Fortin again, not unless Monsieur Yves is here, you understand?' Sylvie nodded again and stealing a sly glance at Marianne's white face, went and fetched the bottle of cognac, pouring a small quantity into a glass and holding it to Marianne's pale lips.

'You have had a shock, *madame*. Come, drink this, it is very good cognac and it will calm your nerves.'

'No! I don't want it.' Marianne pushed the glass aside and reaching for her cup, swallowed hot coffee. 'I've never felt so angry before,' she murmured the words half to herself, then, 'Don't stand there waving that stuff under my nose!' she spoke sharply, an unusual thing for her. 'Drink it yourself or pour it away, I don't want it.' She raised a shaking hand to push away a lock of hair which had fallen across her forehead and tears came to her eyes. 'It's my own fault,' she moaned the words softly. 'All my fault.' Then her voice strengthened. 'Go back to the salon, Sylvie, or wherever you were working. I'll have another cup of coffee and see to lunch. This is one day when I hope Monsieur will not come in for it.'

Sylvie trotted back to the salon, the glass and bottle in her hands. She looked at the small quantity of cognac in the glass and with a smile, filled it up to the brim. Throw away good cognac? Her young face broke into a smile as she sipped at the glassful. It was very good cognac, better than anything she had tasted before. Maman said that Monsieur Yves knew his wines, and Maman was right. After the glass was empty, Sylvie resumed her polishing with increased vigour.

CHAPTER SEVEN

MARIANNE, left alone in the kitchen, put her head down on her arms and allowed the tears to fall. She had been holding them back ever since she had ejected Bernard and her head was now aching as much with suppressed emotion as her mild hangover. By lunchtime she was apparently once more her usual calm self. This was no time for hysterics, she told herself. She must be calm and composed; it would be no good thing if Sylvie went home tonight with a story any more dramatic than was strictly necessary.

Fortunately, when Yves came in for lunch, Sylvie was still busy in the dining room. Marianne faced him across the table.

'Bernard was here this morning,' she spoke conversationally and in English just in case Sylvie came in, which she was bound to do very shortly.

Yves nodded at her. 'Why the English, Marianne? It is something which you don't want the girl to hear?'

Marianne gulped. 'First, Bernard caught me taking two aspirin and suggested that I was using drugs to make life with you tolerable, and when I told him exactly why I was taking two harmless aspirin tablets, he suggested that I was becoming an alcoholic so that I could endure your brutish embraces. I threw him out!' The even tone in which she had been speaking started to wobble. 'Your name is going to be mud in Serac from now on.' Then the hard hold which she had kept on herself was swept away in a rush of tears. 'And it's all my fault,' she wailed. 'That dress last night—I knew what I looked like, I did it deliberately. I didn't want to go shopping in the Land Rover, I wanted you to use the Citroën for that, it's more comfortable.'

Yves was around the table long before she could finish her carefully rehearsed speech and she felt a long, hard arm about her shoulders, an arm which drew her close and felt warm, comforting and quite heavenly.

'So! I drive you to drugs and alcohol, do I?' Marianne raised her eyes to his expressionless face. 'And you threw Bernard out, did you? I commend you! Often I have wished to do just that thing, but always my courage has failed me.'

'It has nothing to do with courage,' she sniffed at him. 'Your manners are probably better than mine.'

'Sylvie, of course, was listening at the door?' He raised an eyebrow and Marianne nodded. Yves looked rueful. 'What a tale she will have to tell when she gets home tonight! We must see that she is on our side, I think.' He put a long finger under her chin, forcing her face up. 'Could you give the impression of a loving and devoted wife?' There was a wry smile mixed up with the intentness of his eyes.

Reluctantly, she gave him a watery smile. 'Camouflage?' she asked as she wiped her wet face on the tea towel.

'Call it that if you wish, Marianne. Now shall we call Sylvie and all have lunch. Since she knows so much of it already, there is no need for any further discussion.' He reached out a finger and wiped away the last trace of her tears. 'Go upstairs and wash your face, madame wife, it will refresh you, and while you are gone, I will have a word with the girl.'

Marianne went upstairs and sponged her face with cold water, re-brushed her hair and put on fresh lipstick. A good impression was so important, so she added a dab of make-up to take away the pinkness at the tip of her nose. Then she hurried downstairs again to hear Yves's voice, deep and serious.

'We must be careful for Madame, it is not good for her to be upset. Not now, in her condition. . . .'

There came an excited squeal and then came Sylvie's fresh young voice assuring him that Madame should be protected in his absence. She, Sylvie, would not permit anything to disturb Madame's serenity at such a time.

Marianne halted on the bottom stair, her hand clutching the newel post. Trust Yves to think of something truly startling! What would Serac make of her after Sylvie had scampered home this evening? After she had regaled her mother with the story of today's doings? An alcoholic hophead and pregnant with it! Her mind started doing sums, mental arithmetic. She was quite definitely not an alcoholic or a drug addict, but pregnant? Now that was quite likely. Once more she did her sums. Of course, it was much too soon to say for sure, but the possibility was there. And how would Yves react to that?

Yves left the house immediately after lunch. A mare in foal was running a temperature and he had to get back to the animal, so that Marianne found herself at Sylvie's tender mercy.

Madame should not stand to wash the dishes, nor should she drag out the heavy old sewing machine. A hot water bottle would be placed in Madame's bed and she should go there and lie down; the little *crise de nerfs* would have exhausted her.

Madame found that surprisingly enough, Sylvie was quite right. She felt very tired indeed and so her resistance to this welcome suggestion was only a token one. Gladly she trotted upstairs and, shedding slacks and jumper, climbed into bed gratefully, where she lay cuddling the hot water bottle, with her feet in the warm place where it had been.

Once again she did her sums and decided, rather despondently, that she could not be sure. But, she brightened, there was every reason to hope. She would like to have a baby, and she fell asleep while deciding which room should be the nursery and how she would decorate it.

'A lazy wife!' Yves's deep voice roused her and she opened her eyes to find him standing by the bed, looking down at her with an odd, hesitant expression. The room was quite dark, it must be at least five o'clock and she had been asleep for three hours. 'I have just run Sylvie home, where she is no doubt broadcasting her news, her breath-taking news.' Yves looked out of the window. 'Would you like to have dinner in Rémy tonight?'

'Why, thank you, kind sir, but if you don't mind, we'll stay at home.' She raised a lazy hand to push back her hair. 'I feel rather languid and it's not a very nice night, is it?' She gestured to the window where rain was already splattering on the panes. 'I have a quiche ready and a Carbonnade Nimoise—mutton to you—which has been stewing nicely for more than three hours. It would be a pity to waste such good food and we could have a quiet evening, unless of course Tante Monique decides to visit us, when we will definitely be going out to dinner in Rémy!'

'As you wish, madame wife.' Yves looked neither pleased or displeased.

'Do you think Sylvie will talk?' she asked.

His eyes flickered over her, taking in her tumbled hair and her face still flushed with sleep, and he grinned sar-donically. 'Freely!' he sat himself on the side of the bed, reaching over to push the hair out of her eyes. 'So will Serac and Tante Monique will be furious. She will see one more obstacle between her and La Barrière.'

'They'll say bad things about you,' she touched his hand briefly, 'and it will be all my fault, but I'll be more careful from now on, I promise. The only tales which Sylvie will be able to carry back will be about a devoted and loving wife. That's the impression I'm going to give from now on. You'll have to help though.'

'Yes,' he smiled down at her in a nasty way. 'You'll need

help for that. You could hardly manage without some co-operation. Don't worry,' he comforted her, 'it won't need much—a few kisses, a tender glance or so. It will be natural enough now that I am an expectant father.'

'You're enjoying this,' Marianne accused. 'I've made an absolute fool of myself and you're enjoying every moment of it!'

'Of course, *ma mie*. How could I not enjoy it? I have always wanted a devoted, loving wife.'

'I didn't say that I would be that sort of wife,' she put the emphasis on the "would". 'I merely intimated that I would give the impression of being one. I'm not a very good actress, though.'

'I thought all women were supposed to be wonderful actresses.' His mouth twisted in a disillusioned smile. 'I'm sure that you could manage a superlative performance if it was necessary.'

Marianne looked at him with an ache in her heart. A superlative performance! Only it wouldn't be acting, it would be for real. 'I'll do my very best,' she said in a dry, humorous tone, and kept her eyes on the bedcover. 'Are you going to co-operate, or are you going to stand on the sidelines and let me do all the work?'

'Did I not say I would co-operate?' His fingers drifted across the smooth skin of her shoulder, tracing the fine line of bone. Under the light touch, she shivered. 'Cold?' He looked very pleased with himself, and she wondered why. 'It is a pity that we do not have a bigger audience, but I'm afraid we shall have to make do with Sylvie and Tante Monique. Between them, they can spread news very efficiently.'

Marianne heard the zoom-zoom of a car changing gear and immediately ran to the window. There was a familiar and friendly note to this particular revving of an engine. Less than a minute later the scarlet and cream TR7 rolled gently into the farmyard and slid quietly to a halt. Liz had come! Marianne felt a great sense of relief. At last she had somebody to whom she could tell her secret, if she wanted to. There was no fun, she had discovered, in having a secret if she was forced to hug it to herself. She did not have to resist the temptation to tell someone because there was nobody to tell. Nobody but Yves! She could tell him, of course, but she had made up her mind that she wouldn't—at least, not yet. Liz was a different kettle of fish.

She opened the door on to the farmyard and waited as Liz's small, debonair figure wriggled its way out of the car and crossed the yard. Liz was bundled up in a variety of woollens and scarves and was shivering as she ran past Marianne and into the house. . . .

'Brr! It's cold. Pleased to see me?' Liz grinned companionably.

'Pleased to see you? I'm delighted!' Marianne hugged the small figure of her friend. 'You're just the person I've been wanting for days.'

'My mental aura,' Liz was mock-modest. 'I came to a dividing of the ways, quite literally. One sign said Clermont, Paris and points north and the other sign pointed west and I found myself going west automatically. Can you put me up?'

'Stupid questions deserve stupid answers,' Marianne smiled at her friend. 'You can sleep in the barn. Come to the fire and get warm.'

'Thanks.' Liz started disrobing. 'The car heater isn't working properly and I've been adding layers to keep myself warm. I've brought your Christmas prezzie, a bit late but better late than never.'

Over coffee in the salon, while Liz thawed out what she called her 'inside bits', Marianne enquired about the Christmas holiday in Switzerland, and Liz gave a running commentary, describing how she and her latest boy-friend came to part.

'He just *stood*! Honestly, Marianne, I've never seen anybody who stood so much! I tried to get him on a pair of skis and he stood while I demonstrated. I tried to teach him the samba and he stood and watched me. Even a simple waltz was too much for him, he stood and gazed at the dancers. If I'd dropped down dead, he would have just stood and watched me, and when I finally waved him goodbye, he stood and watched me out of sight! Talk about Action Man! Oh well,' Liz sighed noisily, 'I'll have to cast my net again.'

'What about Terry?' Marianne asked, remembering the shockheaded, snub-nosed young man who had always been one of Liz's most faithful attendants. She had liked Terry, had found him kind and considerate although a trifle inarticulate. Apart from his inability to string more than three words together at one time, she had always thought him to be one of the better men in the crowd continually circling Liz.

'No!' Liz's answer came violently. 'You know what Terry is? Another racing driver like Jimmy.' Her face grew peaky as she thought of her husband's tragic end. 'I couldn't stand that again.'

'Sorry!' Marianne put out a hand and gently patted her. 'I don't usually interfere, you know that.'

'Good old Marianne!' Liz had quietened down. 'No, you've never interfered, it's one of the most attractive things about you, that quiet patience of yours. Although it has driven me up the wall at times when I've wanted to go out fighting and you've sat quietly, waiting for the right moment! But that's enough about me, now let's have your news. You've been sitting there listening to me rabbiting on and you're bursting with something, I can tell.'

Marianne smiled. 'Not now.' She sniffed and wrinkled her nose. 'I think I can smell something on the point of burning in the kitchen. You go and get your things from the car while I see to lunch and then you'll want to rest.

You must have been driving all night to have arrived here this early. Besides, I want to get my thoughts in order—at the present moment they're in a state of chaos.'

Liz grinned and lay back in the chair. 'Organising Annie disorganised! I refuse to believe it.' She took another sip of coffee and closed her eyes wearily. 'But it's a good idea. I'll rest while you go and do your thing. Wake me when there's something to eat!'

Lunch was over and everything cleared away. Yves hadn't come in for this meal and the two girls and Sylvie had eaten almost in silence since Sylvie spoke no English. In any case, Sylvie was too busy storing up in her mind every detail of Liz's clothing to speak very much. Her mother would be waiting at five o'clock for the latest news from La Barrière and Sylvie also wanted to see the latest hem lengths and styles, something that did not often come her way.

'Go on,' Liz commanded when they were at last alone and the conversation had somehow drifted on to Marianne's recollections of life at La Barrière and the problem of the gossip. 'Don't stop now or I'll go crazy with frustration.'

'But I've told you most of this before,' Marianne objected. 'Why do you want to hear it all over again?'

'The other time, I was just hearing you, I wasn't really listening. It didn't go *in*. This time I'm listening and it's going in now. You say that Gisèle was killed in the car crash—was she alone in the car?'

'I suppose so. I've never heard of anybody being with her.' Marianne wrinkled her brow. 'They would have been hurt as well, it was a very bad crash, and as far as I know there wasn't anyone else hurt, so I suppose she must have been alone.'

'What was Gisèle like? And I don't mean to look at. What sort of person was she underneath?' Liz grinned.

'And in words of not more than two syllables, please. I'm not feeling my best.'

Marianne gazed at the flames in the old range and pushed the coffee pot over to heat. 'Plump,' she said after consideration. 'Plump, white, soft and greedy.'

'Greedy?' Liz raised her eyebrows. 'And she walked out and left all this and the sexy hunk? I don't believe it!'

'Believe it or not, that's what she did. They had a row, she and Yves, and she rushed out just as she was, took the old Fiat and was killed on the hill.'

'Just like that?' Liz sounded sceptical. 'Then please tell me where she was going. The plump, soft, greedy type don't usually leave the nest until they have another nest lined up ready and waiting for them.'

'She need not have been going to anyone,' Marianne demurred.

Liz sighed with exasperation. 'You're judging people by your own standards,' she said. 'It's a bad habit you have. Because you would storm out without even your toothbrush you think that everybody will go and do likewise. Your Gisèle doesn't sound like that type to me. What caused the accident?'

'Road conditions, I should think. It was January and the roads are pretty bad then. They are now.' Marianne moodily twisted the poker, sending another shower of sparks flying up the chimney. 'Anyway, after a while people started talking and hinting that the accident might not have been so accidental. Everybody seems to have known that it wasn't a happy marriage and that there were constant rows, and it started being whispered that Yves could have done something to the van.'

'How convenient!' Liz nodded her flaxen head. 'And after waiting for four years! To me he doesn't look as if he'd put up with anything for four minutes, not if he didn't want to. It's my one accomplishment, you know,' her grin at Marianne was outrageous. 'I know men. I ought to, I've known enough of them,' her blue eyes twinkled ruefully. 'But we're not discussing my murky past. What happened then?'

'Nothing, not for another four years until Grand'mère died. She left a silly sort of will. It wouldn't have held up in a court of law. She left everything between Yves and me, provided we married. If we didn't, Grand'mère said that it all had to go to Bernard.'

'Half a story as usual,' Liz jeered. 'Who is Bernard?'

'You met him last time you were here, don't you remember?' Marianne chuckled. 'You said he looked hungry.'

'Ah, the deep freeze man who wants to go into business with your sexy husband. He came to dinner with his mummy. No, I hadn't forgotten him,' Liz smiled easily. 'I had to unjumble him from half a dozen other hungry-looking young men I've met this holiday. So he was the heir and successor if you and Yves didn't feel in a marital mood.'

'It was quite ridiculous,' Marianne snorted. 'As I said, the will could never have been enforced.'

'Then why did you and he get married?' Liz managed to look innocently bewildered. 'Didn't Yves know about the will not being enforceable?'

'Of course he knew.' Marianne leapt to the defence of her husband and her tone was truculent. 'What do you think he is, a fool? I used to puzzle about it at first because I agreed without thinking about it, without realising that Grand'mère's wishes were merely wishes and not commands.'

'You're in love with him, aren't you?' Liz laid a small firm hand on Marianne's. 'I knew it! So that's your side straightened out. Now for your husband—does he love you?'

'I don't know,' Marianne mumbled. 'I just don't know.'

'O.K.' Liz was brisk. 'Now what else is there?'

Pink-cheeked with embarrassment, Marianne explained about the Land Rover, the black dress and the pale make-up, about Bernard's visit the next morning and the possible gossip about drug addiction and/or alcoholism. When she had finished, Liz was a rolled-up ball of squealing laughter.

Marianne rounded on her friend. 'I don't see what's so funny.' Green sparks glittered in her eyes. 'Yves got hold of Sylvie and said I mustn't be upset in my condition, so Sylvie rushed home with the news and now the village thinks that I'm pregnant as well as all the other things. Yves is laughing his head off.'

'So he's laughing. What's wrong with that? Your Bernard gave them two false premises, what's wrong with your husband starting a third?' Liz looked at Marianne's flushed face. 'Or is that one the Madame? The one that really is true? It is, isn't it? Oh, you great ninny! You're pregnant and you're too scared to tell him, aren't you? When?'

'Another seven months,' Marianne admitted reluctantly. 'But I could be mistaken.'

'Balderdash!' Liz waved away the possibility of any mistake. 'In any case, what do you think you're going to do about it, hug your little secret to yourself until you can put a bonnet on it? It'll be in view for anybody to see in another couple of months.'

'Don't be vulgar! Honestly, Liz, I don't know what to do. One thing I do know, though. I'm not tying Yves to me with a baby, it would be like blackmail, the sort of weapon that Gisèle used.'

'And you're so different from Gisèle, aren't you?' Sarcasm dripped from Liz's tongue. 'Gisèle wanted Yves for a husband, so she pretended to be in the family way. You want him and you're going to pretend that you're not! From what I've seen of your husband, you can stop wriggling, you don't stand a chance. If he doesn't want you he'll throw you out, and if he does want you, you'll not have the chance to get away. Anyway, all this is by the way, your chief problem seems to be the gossip about Gisèle. Have you thought about it? If it was an accident, who started the gossip and why? There's a whole lot of new problems then, like who started the rumours and why, and to answer those questions we'd have to know where she was going and to whom. Beside that little set of conundrums, your coming baby is a minor point.'

'It *was* an accident!' Marianne leapt to the defence of her husband with blazing eyes. 'I know Yves and he wouldn't do a thing like that. And my having a baby isn't a minor point, it's most important.'

'You can come back to England with me and have a little holiday at one of those abortion clinics.' Liz was airy about it. 'Then you could come back here and go on as usual with nobody any the wiser.'

'No!' Marianne was violent. 'No abortion, it wouldn't be fair.'

Liz raised her hands to heaven as if in supplication. 'Give me patience!' she moaned. 'You've lost every bit of common sense you ever had. You're not even reasonable any more—and to think that I used to rely on you! I was the silly one, remember? You were the one with a head stuffed full of brain, all lucid and in perfect going order. I rather like the change, though,' she admitted with a grin. 'It makes me feel superior.'

Marianne stared thoughtfully at the fire, watching the flames lick around the fresh logs she had put on while Liz was talking. Liz was right, she tried to be honest with herself. It did seem as if she wasn't sensible any more. Everything was so mixed up, so involved. She let a little sigh escape her lips. This pregnancy was another complication! No, that wasn't true, she was making it a complication. It all revolved around Yves. She smiled wryly to herself, remembering how she had felt last October. Then she had been content just to have Yves marry her. One step at a time, she had promised herself, but the steps had grown confused and simply being married to Yves had not been enough. She had wanted more, and when he had suggested it, she hadn't been shocked or appalled or even filled with maidenly modesty. She had climbed into his bed without a qualm. She hadn't asked for assurances of love then, she had been blasé about it, so blasé that Yves had thought she was experienced!

While she was preparing the meal, her thoughts went round and round like a treadmill, getting nowhere. If she went away, Yves probably would not come after her and she could not bear the thought of that. If she stayed, as Liz had pointed out, her condition would show and Yves would feel bound. . . . Imprisoned? Bound? Obliged? She couldn't bear that either. There was frustration boiling up in her, she could feel it hot in her chest and dry on the back of her tongue. It made her hand, holding the sharp little vegetable knife, tremble so that the knife slipped and sliced her finger. Dully, she watched the blood well out of the cut until she saw it spotting on the scrubbed table top, then with a brisk 'Tch-Tch' she went across to the sink.

Yves chose this moment to come in, big and windblown, his black hair awry. His hard grey eyes took in the blood on the table and Marianne's hand held under the running tap.

'What are you doing?' he asked.

'I'm committing suicide,' she snapped at him. 'An old Roman custom—one opens a vein and bleeds to death with dignity.'

His reluctant smile broke the severity of his face. 'You have not mastered the technique,' he murmured, reaching for the hand she was holding under the tap and examining the quite small cut on her finger. 'It is necessary, as you said, to open a vein. A small cut such as this would not be sufficient. Why do you wish to commit suicide anyway? Is life so bad?'

'Why do you always take anything I say literally?' she blazed at him. 'You're an infuriating, egoistical man. . . .' She paused for breath, collected herself and went searching in the drawers of the dresser for a tin of plasters which she knew were there somewhere. Yves's hand reached past her to pick up the tin and open it.

'Hold out your hand.' A plaster was expertly applied and the small drip of blood stemmed.

'Liz has called on her way back to England. She's staying a few days—you don't mind?'

'No, I do not mind,' he shook his head. 'Your friends are always welcome, you know that.'

Marianne went back to slicing carrots and cleaning broccoli, stealing a glance at him from under her lashes. Liz had called him a sexy brute and she would go along with the first part of that, but not the second. There was nothing even remotely brutish about Yves Bersac.

The next day, the pale morning sun struggled free of the clouds, but it would not shine for long. More clouds were piling up and the weak winter sun would soon be overcome and hidden once again by cloud and rain.

'What about some shopping?' Liz raised her head from fondling Ludo, who was making a great fuss of her. 'Leave something on a tray for the Lord and Master and we'll go somewhere where there are shops. I'm feeling extravagant. Which reminds me, here is your prezzie. I found it on the back seat of the car. For a while I thought I'd left it in Switzerland—I can never get my packing organised.' Liz produced a box, beautifully wrapped in gold paper and tied up with gold and silver ribbons, the ends of which had been drawn into long curls. She giggled. 'Well, aren't you going to open it?'

'It looks too lovely to spoil.' Marianne continued to admire the wrapping, the neat ends, the curled ribbons. 'I wish I could wrap things like that,' she mourned. 'Here's your present. My parcels always look as if they're going to come apart any moment.'

Liz accepted the small watercolour of Rémy with pleasure. 'I'll hang it as soon as I get back.' She rewrapped it, the curly gold frame making the paper awkward to fasten. 'I'll put it in the cottage, not in the flat.'

The flat which Marianne had Liz had shared in London was an ultra-modern place, open plan, split level, the lot, and though it had been very convenient and comfortable it had always seemed anonymous. The cottage was quite different. Liz and her husband had bought it as a ruin and had spent all their spare time restoring it. It was to the cottage that Liz fled every time her feverish search for a substitute for Jimmy failed. This time, Marianne thought, Liz was not so upset.

Perhaps it had something to do with herself giving Liz an added interest, something to take her mind off her basic loneliness. Marianne was about to muse on this when Liz interrupted her train of thought. 'I shall take Terry down with me when I get back. I'll show him your picture.'

Marianne paused, her fingers fiddling with what looked like an outsize bottle of Chanel No. 5. 'Terry?' she enquired gently.

'Worth a try.' Liz was laconic. 'Old Faithful deserves a little something, don't you think?' She nodded at the unwrapped bottle. 'Did I guess right? Actually it had nothing to do with me, I told the girl that I wanted something for someone elegant and that's what she gave me. You are, you know. You'd look elegant in an old coal sack. Now come on, do! There's an awful lot of good shopping time going to waste.'

Fifteen minutes later the two girls struggled into the scarlet and cream TR7. Marianne wriggled down in the seat and fastened the safety belt.

'Insulting!' Liz commented wryly. 'I'm not going to go that fast.' She started the car and reversed competently to face the open gate of the yard. Sylvie waved to them from the door and Ludo gave a mournful howl of disappointment. The clouds had completely covered the sun by this time and the landscape was grey and dull with rain coming in a fine drizzle. Liz flicked on the windscreen wipers and took the first bend of the hill, throwing up a fine shower of loose chippings into the hedge. Marianne leant back more comfortably in the low bucket seat and was just putting on her sheepskin mitt when Liz said, with a kind of weary fatalism, 'Hang on, ducky. The brakes have gone. It's going to be bit bumpy.'

Marianne looked at the long scarlet bonnet in front of her and then at Liz's small, firm hands grasping the steering wheel. Her mind registered that the knuckles were white and that there was a small chip in the lacquer on one of the nails. They took the second bend on two wheels. Marianne looked at Liz's face. It was white and masklike, but the red mouth was set firm and the blue eyes were hard and cold. The tyres screeched violently as Liz revved and tried to find a lower gear.

'At the next bend,' the words came sharp in Marianne's ear, 'get out of that belt, open the door and jump!'

'Don't be stupid!' Marianne kept it conversational. 'I'm paralysed with fright.' But all the time she was thinking, 'This is how Gisèle felt, she must have been frightened too.' Abruptly her thoughts were brought to an end, the next bend was looming up and Liz, with a careless flip of her wrists, sent the car head-first into the bank.

Marianne heard the screech of metal and the tinkle of glass. There was a savage pain in her chest as the safety belt tightened as she was thrown forward, and then everything went quiet—too quiet. Liz was not moving. In a daze, Marianne unclipped the safety belt and reached over to her friend. 'Liz,' she muttered through lips stiff with fear, and again, 'Liz!' There was no reply. Liz looked as though she had gone to sleep with her head on the steering wheel, her gay woollen cap had fallen off and her blonde hair had swung forward to cover her face.

Painfully Marianne moved in the seat, trying to force the door open, but there was something else she must do first—turn off the ignition. She watched her own hand move slowly across the front of the car and her fingers gripped the ignition key. It was all in slow motion, like an old movie slowed down. The fingers turned the key equally slowly. Now to get Liz out.

With difficulty, she forced the door open against the pressure of a stout branch and swung her legs out of the car, squealing between her teeth in pain and temper because it took so long. Liz was heavy, and somebody as small as Liz had no right to be so heavy. Angrily she tugged and pulled and at last succeeded. They were both outside the car now, and she dragged Liz to what she thought was a safe distance.

Liz was still unconscious and her blonde hair had fallen back to disclose a face masked in blood. Marianne searched for a pulse and found one beating strongly in her friend's neck, and with a sigh of relief she tottered back to the car. The patient must be kept warm. Among the clutter on the back seat was Liz's mink coat, a gorgeous pastel thing with a quilted silk lining. It wasn't as big as a blanket, she thought, but it was probably warmer, and after making a pad of some tissues and binding it round Liz's head with her own scarf, she rolled her up in the furs and sat down to wait.

Now that the accident was over, it was quiet on the hill—too quiet. For a second, Marianne regretted not living beside a four-lane highway, then she scrambled to her feet and went over to the car. For a couple of minutes she threshed about inside and then emerged with a satisfied look on her face. One of Liz's ridiculous red and white stoockings was now tied firmly around the horn button and the air was filled with a raucous bray. It could be heard for miles, she told the unconscious Liz, and it wouldn't stop until the battery ran down. Somebody was bound to hear it and come to investigate. She sat down beside her friend and gathered her close, draping the mink coat over them both.

A touch on her shoulder roused her and she opened her eyes to see Yves looking down at her with a wild anger in his eyes.

'We had a little accident.' The words came slowly as if her mouth was reluctant to say them.

'So I see.' His eyes went over the buckled bonnet of the TR7 and then came to rest on Liz's bloody face. 'Can you walk?'

Marianne nodded at him. 'Of course I can walk,' she said firmly. 'But you'll need transport for Liz.'

'Jacques is coming with the Land Rover.' He was curt, and Marianne subsided into silence. She would have liked to tell him how marvellous Liz had been. If Liz hadn't kept her head, they could both have ended up over the side of the hill and probably dead like Gisèle. Ludo came bounding up and she clutched at his warm body as if it was the only warmth left in the world. Sky, trees, the road and Yves all spun in a crazy circle around her and she felt a hard hand pushing her head down between her knees.

'You can't walk!' Yves sounded even more angry, but somehow it didn't matter any more, and then there was the Land Rover and Jacques taking Liz from her and Yves lifting her into the seat on his knee. Then the tears came and she didn't know why, but Yves's arms were around her and it was very comforting, even if he was in a temper. He carried her up to the bedroom and she stood like a statue while he undressed her and pulled her nightgown over her head.

'Nice,' she mumbled. 'The road was so hard', and with that she drifted off to a nice warm place where there were no rain-soaked hedges scratching at her, no red and cream sports cars and where Liz was not lying on the road with the rain washing blood into a little pink stream that trickled into the ditch.

Some time later she was disturbed by deft hands that moved over her body, and she opened her eyes to see old Dr St Clair leaning over her and beaming behind his thick spectacles.

'*Bien*, *madame*, you wake, and you have no broken bones. Many bruises, but nothing broken.' Marianne nodded and remembered that there was something important which she should ask about, but it didn't seem all that important now. Yves would be coming up soon and he would be spoiling for a fight. She had felt his anger in the road, and it was still there when he had undressed her.

Obediently, she swallowed the small capsule that the doctor put on her tongue, and when she looked up, the doctor was gone and Yves was standing in his place.

'I've just had a pill, so it's no use you standing there and snorting down your nose.' She held on to consciousness with an effort. 'I wasn't driving, and you can thank heaven for that. Liz is a good driver. How is she?'

'Cuts, bruises and shock.' He leaned over her. 'No, as you say, it's useless to say anything to you now.' She looked at him owlishly.

'Just like Gisèle,' she told him. 'No brakes, but Liz is a good driver.' She repeated herself with a faint note of triumph and then, 'I'll quarrel with you tomorrow.' With that, she closed her eyes firmly and went to sleep.

The rattle of a cup in a saucer woke her to a raging thirst and a tearing hunger. Gratefully she accepted the coffee Sylvie was offering. 'I'm hungry,' she wailed, and drained the cup before sliding out of bed. She brushed Sylvie aside when the girl tried to stop her. 'I'm not hurt, Sylvie,' as the girl protested, 'and I must see my friend.' Her legs were wobbly, but every step made them firmer. She found her thick dressing gown and painfully drew it on, wincing as bruised muscles made themselves felt, then, followed by a protesting Sylvie, she made her way down the passage, noting that it was quite dark now. 'What time is it?'

Sylvie muttered that it was six o'clock, but Marianne was pushing open the door into Liz's narrow bedroom. Her only thought was of Liz who was lying in the narrow bed, smiling at her.

'The Oriental Look!' Liz's voice was husky as she gestured towards her bandaged head. 'Tomorrow you can do me a proper turban.'

'Satisfied?' Yves's voice came from behind her and she felt his warm hands holding her shoulders. Marianne turned to the comfort of his arms and the dam holding back her tears burst. She wept all over him, uncaring that her nose was red or that her eyes, between their puffy lids, looked like boiled gooseberries.

'Take her away!' Liz gasped. 'Take her away before she drowns the lot of us. Put her to bed in the bath, it's the safest place!'

Marianne was taken back and put, none too gently, into bed again, and as Yves attempted to tuck her in and Sylvie came running with fresh hot water bottles, she wept on, her hands clinging fiercely about her husband's neck as if he was the only thing stable in a world gone mad. Later she woke to find herself warm in bed. The bedside light was on and she moved painfully. She felt Yves's big warm body beside her and with a sigh of relief she burrowed close against him. His arms held her firmly and she nuzzled her face against his chest. But instead of warm flesh, she felt linen against her cheek.

'You're in bed with your clothes on!' Her voice cracked on a note of disapproval.

'You would not permit me to take them off, *ma mie.*' He sounded amused. 'Do you feel better now? The doctor said that such weeping would be good for you, that it would take away the shock.'

'I'm hungry,' she said plaintively, and he sat up, swinging his legs to the floor.

'Soup,' he suggested.

'And an omelette,' she added quickly. Her eyes encountered the bedside clock and her brows met in a frown. All that time couldn't have passed, surely? The clock could not be right, perhaps it had stopped, but in the silence she could hear its fussy ticking. She looked at Yves ruefully. 'I'm sorry, I've made you miss your dinner. Did you get anything to eat?'

'Sylvie excelled herself.' She saw his lips twitch. 'She charred me a steak. I'll get you your soup now. Madame Liz has already had hers, Sylvie took it in about an hour ago. It was out of a tin, but Madame Liz did not seem to mind. She is asleep now.'

Despite the pain in her chest, Marianne dragged herself upright in the bed. 'I can come downstairs,' she said sturdily. 'I'm not hurt.'

'No?' His fingers pushed aside the strap of her nightgown. 'You are bruised.' He traced the rapidly purpling areas with a gentle finger. 'Stay where you are, Marianne. Take what advantage you can of your injuries. If you had not had them, I would have beaten you. You know the roads are dangerous at this time of the year, but you didn't warn Liz, did you? And don't keep saying that your friend is a good driver, you sound like a parrot. Now I will get you your soup and afterwards, if you still want an omelette, I will cook it for you.'

With a sigh of relief Marianne slid back down into the bed. To be truthful, she felt as weak as a kitten, and she was very glad of somebody to tell her what to do. She was glad too that Yves was so calm, even if he had scolded her when she wasn't up to answering back. Quite a number of her friends would have gone into a flutter if they had had to cope with an accident and two battered women. Yves took it in his stride, hardly turning a hair.

She was not sure whether this attitude was a good thing or not, considering that his wife was one of the battered women. Would she have liked it better if he had appeared a little upset? This problem occupied her mind until he reappeared with her soup and then hunger drove everything else from her mind. Perversely, when she had finished the soup, she was too tired to eat anything else, but not too tired to think.

'Sylvie?' she croaked.

'Asleep in the salon.' Yves was actually smiling at her. 'In case she is needed during the night. She says that the sofa is most comfortable, better than the bed which she shares with her mother. Ludo is also asleep. Have you any more enquiries about your household, madame wife?'

Marianne said, 'No.' She would have shaken her head, but the movement caused a deal of pain, and that was something she could do without, and with a sigh, she drifted off to sleep, wishing that Yves would smile more often. But then he hadn't an awful lot to smile about, poor darling. She said it aloud, 'Poor darling', and felt the arms about her tighten comfortingly.

CHAPTER EIGHT

ALTHOUGH Marianne was up and about on the day following the accident, it was three whole days before Liz would allow herself to be helped downstairs. At first she snorted defiance at Marianne.

'Let anybody see me looking like this?' She pointed to her bruised face and the ugly stitches at her temple where a small portion of her hair had been cut off. 'Nobody is going to see me until my black eye has gone and the doctor has taken out these revolting stitches. You'd think they would use flesh-coloured thread, wouldn't you?'

Marianne shook up another pillow and stuffed it behind her friend's back. 'You lóok wonderful to me,' she frowned. 'It still feels like a miracle that we're both alive. When I pulled you out of that car I thought for one horrible moment that you were dead and the most beautiful thing in the world at that time was the jump of your pulse.'

Liz chuckled. 'Have you thought about it? Here we are, for the first time in our lives sick women, and do people come visiting, bringing us flowers and grapes and tender sympathy, and could we wallow in it, if we got any? No, because both of us look as though we've been in the ring with Muhammed Ali. Yours doesn't show so much, which is lucky for you.'

'As for your bruises and the stitches,' Marianne looked at her friend consideringly, 'your make-up case is here. I'm sure you could do something about your face and you could cover those stitches if you brushed your hair back and wore a scarf around your head, or tied it back with an Alice band. That would cover the stitches easily.'

'What it is to be born with brains! Be a doll and find me something to wear while I remove the worst with pancake make-up.' Once started, Liz wasted no time, so that a little more than an hour later the bruising was hidden under a thick layer of make-up and the stitches were concealed by a wide, soft Alice band. Liz gave a satisfied grunt and laid down the hand mirror to look at Marianne for approval. Marianne grinned.

'It hardly shows at all, and with your hair like that, you look about seventeen.'

Liz grinned back. 'That's what I like about you, what I've always liked.' She consulted the mirror again. 'You don't stint your praise. A lot of my feminine friends would have been milk-and-waterish about it. They would have suggested that I sit in a dark corner or wear a veil, but not you. You tell me it won't show and I believe you. You're good for my morale!'

Marianne tossed on to the bed the cream woollen smock which Liz had bought from Madame Jeanne's before Christmas. 'How about that?' she asked. 'It's very becoming, it suits you and it will be comfortable. You don't want anything fitted on your first evening downstairs. And now let's hurry. It's taken an age to do your face.'

Liz was wriggling the dress over her head and from within the folds her voice came muffled. 'That's why you think I look seventeen,' she pushed her head through the neckline of the dress. 'It takes some doing, covering up my battered look *and* losing fifteen years at the same time!'

Yves carried Liz downstairs and placed her on the couch, where she reclined looking like a blonde edition of David's Madame Récamier. 'Now all I need is a big thick steak smothered in mushrooms. It is steak I can smell, isn't it?' Liz enquired hungrily.

'Steak it is,' Marianne chuckled weakly. 'Don't make me laugh too much, there's enough pain in my chest already.' Anxiously she surveyed her friend and breathed a sigh of relief. In the soft golden light from the standard lamp, Liz looked her usual beautiful self.

'Dinner by candlelight, please,' Liz demanded. 'It's so much more flattering, and in our present weakened state, Marianne and I need all the flattery we can get. Sherry! How lovely.' she accepted the glass from Yves. 'Now I know I'm in France! No British doctor would allow us alcohol, not in our bruised and battered condition.' She sipped appreciatively. 'Mmm, nice and dry. Do you know, I think I feel better already, and I'm sure I could totter as far as the dining room under my own steam if somebody walks closely behind me, just in case of accidents.'

Back in the salon after dinner, Liz turned innocent blue eyes on Yves. 'My car?' Marianne felt a chill draught and looked to see if a door had been left open. None had, of course. She knew that even before she turned her head. It wasn't a draught either, it was the knot of fear that was uncoiling itself in her stomach and spreading cold tentacles right through her body. She grew angry with herself and even a little angry with Liz.

It had been such a lovely evening so far, so why did Liz have to make one little remark that spoiled it all? Then her common sense reasserted itself. Liz wasn't accusing anybody, she was asking a perfectly normal question, the sort of question that anybody would ask in these circumstances. If the car was a write-off, then Liz would have to find some other means of transportation back to England. It was she, Marianne, who was reading into an innocent question more than had been intended. It just showed the state she had allowed herself to get into. Mentally Marianne scolded herself.

'It was towed down to the garage in Serac,' Yves volunteered, his face impassive. He had been smiling over dinner, listening to Liz's caustic banter and her graphic descriptions of life among the jet set in Switzerland. Liz had been exhibiting all the resilience of a rubber ball, bouncing back to her normal self after the accident, with a little something added, Marianne thought. The gaiety did not seem as feverish and her blue eyes were warmer. But now, behind the innocence, Liz's eyes were cold once more. Cold and determined. Lost in her own thoughts, Marianne missed some part of the conversation and when she dragged her mind back to it, it was to hear Liz say, 'The brakes failed. I would like a written report from the mechanic on that.'

Marianne found herself thinking about another accident where the possible cause had been brake failure and which had not ended so happily. The shiver of cold crept up her spine once more and just for a second it seemed that Liz, lounging on the couch, was no longer Liz but Gisèle. She closed her eyes. It was imagination, she told herself sternly. A combination of circumstances. The similarity of colouring between Gisèle and Liz, because actually they were quite unalike if one discounted the fair hair and blue eyes. There was nothing about Liz that could remind her of Gisèle's plump, well-fed laziness. When she opened her eyes again it was to see Liz calmly lighting another cigarette.

'I'll have to put in an insurance claim,' Liz was saying, 'so there will have to be a sort of inquest on my dead car, and the more evidence I can supply, the easier it will be for me.'

Yves nodded his black head in agreement. 'Then in that case, Madame Liz, we shall have to have the car towed to either Rémy or Clermont. Henri is very old, so old that the insides of modern cars are quite beyond him. He changes plugs and greases and when needed acts as a driver, but that is all. I suggest that you leave everything until you are well enough to see for yourself, then I will arrange to have the car towed wherever you say.'

'It's a pity it's a write-off,' Liz mourned, 'I liked that car, but I suppose I can hire something to get me back to the Channel port. It will be easier in England.' She chuckled. 'I'll leave all the hiring to you—with my French I'd probably end up with a donkey and a cart, and I can't drive a donkey!'

'You have a very businesslike mind, Madame Liz.' There was amusement in Yves's voice.

'Yes, I have, haven't I?' Liz grinned at him amiably. 'I'm so glad you noticed it. Everyone else treats me as if I hadn't an ounce of brain, and it's very humiliating.'

Marianne listened to this byplay and then jumped up swiftly, the sudden movement making her skirt swirl out and catch the fire tongs, which fell to the hearth with a resounding clatter.

'I don't know about you, Liz, but I feel I've been up

long enough.' She stifled a yawn. 'Can you manage the stairs?'

'Yes, I could,' answered Liz, adding reflectively with a small gurgle of laughter running through the words, 'but I'd much rather be carried. It's so romantic and it makes me feel very precious.'

Yves's mouth curved in a reluctant smile. 'At your service, *madame*.'

'Make it Liz.' Blue eyes sparkled with laughter. 'All this 'Madame' business makes me feel like the keeper of a bawdy house!' Halfway up the stairs, she peeped at Marianne over Yves's shoulder. 'I like your husband, darling. You wouldn't care to share him, would you?'

'*No*!' Marianne laughed as well as her bruising would permit. 'Get one of your own, you've got a wide choice.'

Just as she was getting into bed, some devil prompted her. 'You've made quite a hit with Liz.' She said the words to her husband's back as he was shedding his dressing gown. 'Perhaps she's the sort of woman you should have married. Full of *joie de vivre* and with a quick answer to everything.'

'But I married you, Marianne.' He looked down at her sombrely.

'Perhaps you shouldn't have,' she pressed the point. 'You might have been better off with somebody who could make you laugh.'

'I am very well satisfied with the wife I have.' The bed stirred as he slid into it and then there was the snap of the switch as the light went out. 'And when your bruising has become less painful, I shall be even better satisfied.'

'I can't help thinking. . . .'

'Marianne,' he turned to face her in the darkness, 'you think too much.' He pulled her close and she winced with the pain of it and was glad it hurt so much. Yves swore fluently. 'Go to sleep, madame wife. It is far too late for you to be worrying about the sort of woman I should have married. When I have any complaints, I will let you know.'

Halfway through the next week, Dr St. Clair came and removed the stitches from Liz's head wound and his patient crowed with delight, meanwhile telling the doctor in execrable French that he should use thread that did not contrast so greatly with the background, horrid black stuff that it was. It was all right for men who loved to be able to show off their injuries and have loads of fuss made over them, but for females, who only wanted to look good, black sewing was abhorrent! The doctor twinkled behind his thick spectacles. His advanced years did not stop him appreciating a beautiful woman, especially one who combined beauty and wit. Flesh-coloured stitches, he pointed out, would blend with the background and therefore might be missed and then prove troublesome. Liz batted her eyelashes and the doctor twinkled back at her before trotting off to see Marianne in private.

'Yes,' he nodded at her. It seemed likely that her suspicions were correct. It was a trifle early, he thought, to make a definite diagnosis, but the small signs were there. Another few weeks, perhaps only days, and Madame Bersac could be sure.

Madame Bersac, who had been measuring herself zealously with a tape measure for the past five days, sighed and ground her teeth with frustration.

At this the old doctor shook his head. Frustration, worry of any kind was bad for the system at a time like this. How could the body concentrate on this new life if the mind was busy with other things? What was necessary now was for Madame to relax, to be happy, contented, a vegetable for a while.

When he had gone, Marianne prowled about the house like a displaced person. Relax! How could she relax when Liz's sparkle had turned to the hard diamond glitter of old?

When Yves was being the perfect host, urbane but uncommunicative?

She was deft now about the work in the office. When the post came, she opened it and sorted it, typing out replies to the letters she was certain of and making a neat pile of the ones which required Yves's attention. She had instituted a new filing system and had blushed with pleasure when Yves complimented her on her work. She had also learned a lot more about La Barrière and the vineyard, far more than she had ever known when she lived here before.

A great deal of work originated from the vineyard. She had blinked with surprise at first, but a quick look at the map on the office wall showed that it was a very big one and from the lightly shaded areas around it, each one marked with the name of its present owner, it looked as if Yves intended to extend it farther as and when the plots became available.

She was amused and touched by the scrupulous honesty of Yves's bookkeeping. Apparently the vineyard had never been part of La Barrière, it had come to Yves from his mother, and the farm and vineyard were run as two separate concerns. The profits from one were never used to bolster up the other and all the accounts tallied to the sou. Happily, Marianne tapped away on her beautiful new typewriter. It was useful work she was doing, she thought. Even Bernard's venture into the frozen meat business had been meticulously costed. The profits from it would be considerable, but Yves did not need them. According to the accounts and bank statements, he was already a very wealthy man.

Liz put her head round the door. 'Busy little bee, aren't you? With talents in all directions! You're able to run a house, cook like an angel and perform on that idiot machine. Is there anything you can't do?'

'Lots,' Marianne smiled, trying to inject a little humour into the word. 'I can't wear size three shoes or size ten clothes and I'm useless with a spanner. The list is endless. You've been like a cat on hot bricks for nearly a week—what's the matter?'

'Since you're here and obviously aware of my nervous condition,' Liz lit a cigarette, fumbling with the lighter, 'I will unburden myself. Everything shall be revealed! I did a mad thing, Marianne, and now I'm paying for it.' Marianne's face expressed her bewilderment and Liz studied the tip of her cigarette with deep concentration. 'I wrote to Terry,' she mumbled, studiously avoiding Marianne's eyes. 'I offered myself,' she continued with sad bravado. 'I drew his attention to my rather sullied past and promised to be a good girl in future if he would share that future with me. I wasn't myself after the accident, you know. I went all soft!'

Marianne breathed a sigh of relief. For several days now she had been cultivating the idea that Liz had fallen for Yves; she seemed so right for him. It was to Liz that Yves made humorous remarks and it was with Liz that Yves laughed. She had been worrying about nothing again. 'Why the sudden change?' She rose from her seat and came to put her arm about Liz, who was angrily stubbing out her cigarette.

'I've always said that I didn't want to live without Jimmy.' Liz raised a woebegone face. 'But when the brakes failed and I knew we were going to crash, I suddenly discovered that I quite definitely didn't want to die. So I wrote that damnfool letter and I haven't had a reply. All I can think of is Terry sitting somewhere and gnawing at the end of his ball point, thinking up ways to say "No" without hurting my feelings.' Liz looked out of wide blue shamed eyes and raked through her hair with shaking fingers. 'It's all your fault,' she glared at Marianne. 'I came here and you gave me a demonstration of married life. Oh, I know it's far from perfect, you don't have to tell me that, but from where I'm standing on the outside, it looks pretty good. Anyway, I fell for it. I wanted some too, so I wrote that letter and put myself right behind the eight ball. I must have a hole in my head!'

Marianne hugged the narrow shoulders. 'You're a pathetic little idiot,' she said with warmth. 'A pathetic, proud little idiot. Come and have some coffee and talk to me while I start tonight's meal.'

'What are we having?' Liz started to look interested.

'A *daube.*'

'What on earth's that?' Liz made a moue of distaste. 'It sounds revolting.'

Marianne laughed at the expression on Liz's face. 'It won't taste revolting,' she promised. 'It's a Provençal dish originally, a sort of stew.' Liz started to look doubtful again and Marianne hastened to reassure her, 'You'll like it, I'm sure. I believe the only thing you know about French cooking is coq au vin.'

'I know boeuf bourguignon,' contradicted Liz, 'but I can't spell it and I know that chicken thing that Napolean's chef threw together after a battle.'

'Chicken Marengo? A *daube*'s nothing like that. It's a farmhouse dish, thoroughly provincial. We'll have rice with it.'

After coffee, Liz sat and watched with interest as Marianne chopped and prepared meat and vegetables, cutting pork rinds into one-inch squares and beef into postcard-sized slices, chopping onions and carrots, skinning tomatoes and then arranging the whole lot in a wide earthenware pot with the meat on top. She crowed with delight as Marianne swirled boiling wine in a small saucepan and set light to it deftly before pouring it over the gently cooking meat and vegetables, and stuffed a bouquet garni in the layer below the meat before putting the now covered pot in the oven of the old range.

'I wish I could cook,' she said enviously. 'But I'm hopeless. I've only to see a saucepan and I start shaking with fright. What's for afters?' she enquired greedily. 'I loathe those caramel cream things. Couldn't we have rice pudding? My mother used to make gorgeous rice pudding, we ate it with a big dollop of redcurrant jelly on the top.'

They were disturbed at dinner by the sound of the telephone. Marianne's lips tightened. Bernard, she supposed, wanting to come for further clarification on his frozen meat. She wished he'd start doing something instead of forever asking questions. She didn't want him, or his mother either. They would bring the gossip and rumours from Serac Ste. Marie with them, spoiling everything.

Yves wasn't long. He came back to the dining room almost immediately. 'A telephone call for you, Madame Liz, from England.' Liz looked at him as if he was speaking Chinese. Yves repeated, 'A telephone call for you, from England. Don't you want to answer it?' He returned to his chair and smiled at Marianne. 'A very expensive call, and Madame Liz keeps him waiting—a Monsieur Terry Canby.'

Liz flew out of the room as if she was jet-propelled and Marianne rose.

'I'll fetch the pudding,' she murmured the words softly with the feeling that if she had yelled them at the top of her voice, nobody would have paid any attention to her. Then she went to the door, grabbing Yves by the arm and dragging him with her.

'Give her a little time,' she pleaded. 'Dinner won't spoil for waiting a few minutes. I suppose I should start putting hot water bottles in the second spare room bed. Terry's very dogged, he's bound to come to fetch her. We shall have to find him a bed for a couple of days.'

'Will that be necessary?' Yves sounded cynical and Marianne glared at him.

'It's easy to see that you never slept in what used to be my bed,' she retorted tartly. 'It's much too narrow for more than one person.' Wrath rose in her. 'You're despicable!' she hissed. 'Do you have to bring everything down to the level of a—a bordello?' She hesitated over the last word, hoping it was the correct name, it sounded lascivious enough. In fact she was quite pleased with it, and she faced her husband with a fighting gleam in her eyes.

'The cat spits.' He was unrepentant. 'Don't try your claws on me, madame!'

Marianne suppressed with difficulty an almost overwhelming desire to wipe the mockery from his face with a good hard slap. Instead she contented herself with the query, 'Jealous?'

'Jealous?' He raised his eyebrows at what he seemingly thought her incredible stupidity. 'No, Marianne, not jealous at all. Why should I be? Do I not have a beautiful, charming, loving wife?'

'I bet you say that to all the girls!' she muttered, half under her breath, and then turned on him. 'I don't know about this beautiful, charming wife you have—are you by any chance a bigamist? Because you can't possibly be talking about me!'

'Oh, but I am talking about you, Marianne.' His mockery became more evident as his eyes slid over her. 'Beautiful? Yes. Charming? When you want to be. Loving? There are some things that even you cannot hide.' He gave a short, hard laugh.

'Bastard!' she spat the word at him and felt her arm seized and the grip tighten.

'I have told you before,' he warned, 'I do not care to hear such words from your lips. They do not become you, and I will not have my wife using gutter language.'

'And what will you do?' she jeered. 'Beat me?'

'No, I do not think that beatings are the answer. There are other, more pleasant ways of punishment,' he allowed a small, cruel smile to touch his mouth. 'Do not look so stricken, Marianne. Did I not say that they were pleasant ways?'

Suddenly she shook herself, taking a breath, a deep one. 'Would you mind telling me what we're quarrelling about? I'm at the stage of thoroughly losing my temper and I can't even remember how it all started.' She was finally jerked out of her bad humour when Yves burst into laughter.

'God knows. I don't recall the origin myself, but I must confess that it is very pleasant to see you animated once again. Since the accident you have been something like a shop window model, except that you squeak when I touch.'

'I've been sore.' Marianne put a hand to her ribs. 'You saw for yourself how much bruising there was. I'm only grateful that it was no worse, we could have been much more seriously hurt, in fact, I think we got off very lightly, but even this small amount of damage is still very painful.' She grimaced slightly and added as an afterthought, 'I think I'm still a little bit shocked.'

'And suspicious, perhaps?' He raised an eyebrow in mute query. 'I watched you when Madame Liz and I spoke of the car. You looked like a Christian being fed to the lions, and the look of relief on your face when you found Madame Liz was thinking about insurance claims was comical. Did you think that I had engineered another accident, perhaps?'

'No! I think nothing of the kind.' Her eyes sparked with anger. 'How dare you think that. . . .' Marianne extricated herself from the knot into which she was tying herself and started again. 'It's not a matter of what I think, is it? It's what they're thinking and saying down in Serac.'

'You care what they think and say?' Yves sounded incredulous and his hand reached out to take hers.

'Not for myself.' She allowed her cold fingers to lie in his warm grasp. 'They can't say anything about me except that I'm all sorts of a fool, and I don't care about that, but they won't be talking about me, will they? They'll be talking about you.' She was struck by a sudden thought and gave it voice. 'It was a good job that both Liz and I were in the car. If it had been me, on my own, the tongues in Serac would have had a field day. Think what they would have made of that! You would probably have been accused of trying to get rid of me to make room for Liz in your bed.'

'Give a dog a bad name!' Yves chuckled, and the sheer lightheartedness of it made her smile, although it was a very reluctant little smile. 'They will have something else to talk about now, won't they? The arrival of another man will cause quite a furore. I wonder whether they will allot him to Madame Liz or will they perhaps assume that he is a contender for your favours.'

'Don't be disgusting!' she snorted at the very idea.

'Disgusting? I see nothing disgusting in a man wanting my wife. It is surely a compliment to my good taste.' He was being outrageous, Marianne decided, and her colour rose as he continued, 'Now, if my wife wanted another man, that would be a different matter.'

'Then it's a good job I don't.' Marianne brought the conversation to an end quickly, it was getting out of her depth and making her feel embarrassed. Yves was not to be so easily put off.

'Was there no man in London? Don't tell me that they all went around with closed eyes when you were present—I would not believe that.'

'I was far too busy,' she said flatly, and made for the kitchen door with the large dish of rice pudding. 'I hope you like this,' she flung the words over her shoulder. 'I made it especially for Liz, she remembers it from when she was a child, and I hunted and found a jar of redcurrant jelly to serve with it.'

Liz had returned to the dining room when Marianne

came in with the rice pudding. She was seated at the table with a stunned look on her face and a faraway light in her blue eyes.

'He's been in the States and didn't get my letter until this evening.'

'And?' Marianne set the dish on the table and resumed her seat.

'He's going to phone tomorrow after he's made the arrangements to come for me. He says I'm not to think of driving myself, not so soon after an accident.' Liz heaved a huge sigh of satisfaction.

Marianne looked at her friend and then, pointedly, at the rice pudding. 'I made this specially for you,' she was severe. 'If you're going to sit there with that "gone away" look in your eyes, and not eat it, I shall throw it all over you!'

Liz came down from cloud nine with a visible effort. 'What is it?' she asked vaguely, and then, 'Rice pudding *and* redcurrant jelly! Lovely! I'm awfully hungry.'

Terry Canby arrived three days later and in the nicest possible way organised Liz into departing within twenty-four hours of the time of his arrival.

'I daren't leave it too long,' he told Marianne engagingly. 'Liz might change her mind, so the sooner I get her back to London the better. I'll just see to the business about her car, collect statements from you about the accident and get a report on the car from the garage and we'll be off.' Thus Terry, who had only been in the house for an hour, arranged Liz's immediate future, and Liz sat and looked at him as if he was some superior being from outer space. Well, she had always wanted somebody to look after her!

When the salon fire had burned down to a pile of feathery grey ash, Marianne professed herself ready for bed. Liz and Terry had retired much earlier. Terry explained that they would have a busy day ahead of them and, unlike Liz, he found no fault with his narrow bed in the equally narrow, monastic room. He grinned engagingly. He would have found no fault with a bale of hay in the barn, and he smiled a very sweet, sleepy smile.

When they had gone, Yves looked at his wife with irritation. She was half asleep in the chair. 'I'm tired,' she told him drowsily. 'I'll go to bed, I think,' but she made no effort to rise, instead she allowed her eyes to close sleepily and sat up, blinking, when he touched her shoulder. 'Sorry,' she murmured. 'I must have dozed off, it's been a long day.'

'I would be better pleased if you did less work,' he told her with exasperation.

Marianne dragged herself to her feet and glowered at him. 'Thank you,' she said through a wide yawn. 'That's helpful, telling me what I can do to please you. What I mean is that if ever I did want to please you, I'll know just how to go about it, won't I?'

'Little cats that spit get slapped,' he glowered back at her, his hand hard about her arm. Then his voice lost its abrasive quality. 'Come to bed, *ma mie* and in future, allow Sylvie to do more.'

'She's little more than a child,' she protested.

'Try telling that to Sylvie, or Jacques either for that matter,' he laughed in what Marianne thought was a very nasty way. 'Sylvie has not been a child for several years.'

'Either you've a foul mind, Yves Bersac, or you have personal experience,' Marianne muttered the comment in a low voice, but not low enough. His ears caught it and the hand on her arm tightened painfully.

'Have I not warned you about spitting cats?' Yves's grey eyes were hard and his mouth a thin line of displeasure. 'I also told you, before we were married, that I did not find my pleasures in the village. That was the truth, madame wife. I do not tell unnecessary lies.'

Marianne made an unsuccessful attempt to free herself

from his painful grasp. 'What comes under the heading of necessary lies?' she snapped. 'The sweet nothings you tend to murmur in bed?'

'That is for you to decide. Whatever your verdict, I will abide by it.' His smile was far from pleasant. 'How could I contradict my beautiful, charming and loving wife?'

'Haven't we been into that before?' she snorted down her small, straight nose.

'Have we?' He pushed her towards the stairs. 'In any case, it is too late to develop the argument tonight.'

As he closed the bedroom door behind him, Marianne emerged from the wardrobe where she had been tidily hanging up the long velvet skirt she had been wearing that evening. It would have been so nice, she thought, to have been able to leave it and the rest of her clothes in a heap on the floor or draped over the back of a chair as Liz was wont to do, but years of training could not be overcome so easily. Yves commented on her ingrained tidiness.

'But for your brush and comb on the dressing table, *ma mie*, I do not think that anyone would ever suspect that you shared this room with me. There is not one feminine touch about it.'

She slipped out of her robe and hung it over the end of the bed, put her slippers neatly by the bedside and eased herself into bed before she answered him.

'You complained of a feminine invasion of the bathroom,' she reminded him. 'Feminine fripperies, you called them, and said it smelled like a harem.' She snuggled down in the bed and turned her back on him. 'There's no pleasing some people.' St Catherine, strapped to her wheel, could not have spoken in a more martyred tone, and she closed her eyes in resignation.

She felt the bed depress as Yves slid beneath the covers and a warm hand came hard on her shoulder, turning her from her curled-up position on to her back. Releasing her shoulder, he put up a hand to stroke back her hair from her face, and he sounded amused as he asked, 'Are you going to squeak if I hold you tonight?'

Marianne kept her eyes shut and her face expressionless. She was upset, she told herself. He had threatened to slap her and he had suggested that Sylvie . . . and it was going to take more than a deep caressing voice to restore her to anything like good humour. Then at the touch of his hands, her thoughts were in turmoil. It was so difficult to preserve a nonchalant attitude when Yves was in this mood. He shook her gently when she did not answer him and she felt his breath against her skin.

'Don't pretend you didn't hear me, Marianne. Even you could not fall asleep as quickly as that.' He nuzzled her shoulder, pushing the narrow strap of her nightgown aside. Marianne heaved a sigh and gave up the unequal contest. She could not fight herself and him as well. She opened her eyes and allowed one arm to slide up around his neck. It was going to do so anyway, she comforted herself, so what was the use of struggling? His mouth came down swiftly on her own, warm, demanding and hard. At last, when her mouth was free, she gasped for breath and pleaded, 'Please put out the light.'

'But I want to see your face,' he murmered the words against the skin of her throat.

'No!' She turned her head away, only to have it turned back again swiftly.

'Why may I not see your face when I make love to you?' His hands were stroking, soothing caressing. 'Why do you try to hide from me? Can it be that you wish to close your eyes and think of England, is that what you are going to do now?'

'No!' Rash words spilled from her mouth, words she would never have dared to say if he hadn't teased her into saying them. 'I'm going to enjoy it! You seem to, so why shouldn't I? Please put that light out.'

'Anything to oblige you, *ma mie*.' There was a small click

and in the ensuing darkness she heard Yves's soft chuckle. 'Do I rip this nightgown? You objected before, but it's either rip nightgowns or strangle you, and nightgowns are expendable, whereas you, my Marianne, are quite unique.'

'*Merci du compliment.*' Some of his good humour seemed to have washed off on to her, for she found herself smiling in the darkness. She wished his good humour was a little more predictable, though. His moods seemed to change with great rapidity.

'Marianne?' It came as a soft query in the darkness and she slid her other arm around his neck to pull his head down to hers. Why not? she asked herself. She was doing nothing to be ashamed of. This man was her husband—and then his mouth and hands stopped all her thoughts as they filled her with a desperate need and she found herself clinging to him urgently, finding in him a need as desperate as her own. She felt herself melting, flowing, until they were no longer two separate people but were somehow joined. Dimly she heard Yves speaking and with an effort she concentrated on what he was saying. 'Marianne, Marianne,' just her name, over and over again as if it was some sort of spell he was chanting. She laughed softly and wound her arms more tightly about him.

The skin of his shoulders was satiny smooth under her fingertips and she traced the line of the bones and muscles with a feeling of discovery. Her mouth tasted the salt on his skin and she felt his body move against hers. Her eyes closed in a secret delight. This was an emotion he couldn't counterfeit, surely? She felt drugged with pleasure and sighed against his mouth. She heard his soft laugh of triumph and didn't care. He could make her feel like this, and all she wanted was to be able to give him as much pleasure as he was giving her. And then there was no more room for thought, no room for anything except being as close to him as she could get.

CHAPTER NINE

'*Bonjour, madame.*' Sylvie's young voice, bright with excitement, woke Marianne from a lovely dream where she and Yves were wandering through some sort of Paradise and Yves had just told her that he worshipped the ground she trod on. That was how she knew it was a dream. In ordinary, everyday life, her husband would never indulge in such a weakness. Now here was Sylvie to bring her back to earth.

Marianne turned her face into the pillow. Why could she not be satisfied with what she had? It wasn't so bad really, and she guessed that it was a great deal more than many other women ever achieved. But it would be nice. . . . Oh no, it was not the slightest use indulging herself in fantasy, in useless, silly daydreams. Determinedly she turned to find bright daylight streaming through the window. At least it wasn't raining.

Sylvie chirrupped with the joy of youth and darted about the room, drawing curtains, beating pillows to death and obviously bursting with curiosity. Marianne smiled at her and Sylvie smiled back.

'I brought extra bread and croissants this morning, *madame*, for Jacques told me that you have another visitor.'

Marianne closed her eyes in resignation. It was just like living in a goldfish bowl! There was nothing that could be hidden from the good people of Serac. There was nothing else to do but to satisfy their curiosity, and the best way of doing that was to give Sylvie the information she was so obviously seeking.

'An Englishman,' she said as she sipped hot coffee from the cup which Sylvie handed her. 'The fiancé of Madame

Liz, who has come to take her back to England since her own car is wrecked.'

'*Bien sur.*' Sylvie was, as ever, in a receptive mood, and Marianne was quite certain that every word she said would be taken home and faithfully reproduced for the benefit of Madame Berthilot and such of her friends as were waiting for the titbits of gossip trembling on the tip of Sylvie's tongue that evening.

'Such a man!' Sylvie paused in the act of taking the empty coffee cup, her whole figure one gigantic question mark.

Marianne smiled again at this so obvious thirst for information and decided that she had better satisfy it. Otherwise, she thought, who knew what tales would be travelling from house to house in the village by nightfall.

'He is a very famous racing driver and has just come back from the United States of America. He has a great *tendresse* for Madame Liz, indeed he has loved her for many years, and at last they are to be married.'

Sylvie heaved a romantic sigh at this last piece of information and imparted another piece of information in exchange for it. 'He and Monsieur Yves speak of going to the garage in Serac, but to what purpose, *madame*? The car of Madame Liz will never be driven again, Jacques has told me this. It is too badly damaged.'

Marianne allowed herself a bright, gay smile. It did not reach as far as her eyes, but she kept it firmly pinned on her lips while her mind swiftly assessed the possibilities of her next words. She could either turn the conversation into a new channel and thereby divert Sylvie's train of thought temporarily, she could give a little shrug and start the girl's imagination working overtime, or she could tell the truth and let the village draw its own conclusions—or perhaps she could do better than that! Sylvie broke in on this short silence which she evidently took to mean that Marianne was as mystified as she was.

'The car is quite smashed, *madame*,' her head nodded vehemently. 'What good can come of looking at a smashed car?'

Marianne paddled her feet under the bed, searching for her slippers while she shrugged on her dressing gown. When the sash had been firmly knotted about her waist, she turned back to Sylvie, who was standing with the empty coffee cup in her hand, still waiting to hear what Marianne thought.

'Madame Liz is not satisfied that the car was examined by old Henri at the garage. It is a question of the insurance, for Madame Liz to claim the full amount she will need a certificate from a mechanic. Henri cannot give her that, therefore the car must be taken to Rémy or Clermont. That is what Monsieur Yves and the fiancé of Madame Liz go to arrange.' She felt rather pleased with her reply. It was true, and more than that, it would be just the way any practical Frenchman would think. Insurance and money. They would understand that!

Sylvie digested the information hungrily and went back to the kitchen where she would no doubt spend the next half hour or so in frustrated misery because Terry spoke no French and Yves would be speaking English, a language with which Sylvie was quite unacquainted.

Less than half an hour later, Marianne joined Sylvie and started to set the table for breakfast. They would have it in the kitchen, she decided, since the dining room had not yet had the benefit of Sylvie's ministrations and the fire there had not yet been lit, whereas the kitchen was wonderfully warm. It was very satisfying, she thought, to see the look of happiness on Liz's face as she drifted in, looking as beautiful as ever, wrapped her arms about Terry's not inconsiderable form and planted a smacking kiss on his mouth. Sylvie hovered like a piece of blotting paper, mopping up every little action so that it could be recalled and recounted later.

'Morning, everybody!' Liz looked at Terry's flushed face with concern. 'Are you sickening for something, or have I embarrassed you?'

'It's going to take a bit of getting used to,' admitted Terry, 'but I think I'll get used to it if you give me time. I've never had this sort of treatment before and it's bound to make me feel embarrassed for a while!'

Liz hooted with laughter, recalling several incidents when he had been garlanded with laurel wreaths and completely submerged beneath a pile of ardent and excited young women. Terry blushed again and defended himself.

'It's none of my doing if there are half a dozen photographers present and everybody wants to get in on the act,' he mumbled selfconsciously, before turning to Yves. 'Do you have this trouble with Marianne?'

'No trouble at all.' Yves spoke in English and Marianne watched Sylvie's eyes grow wide and disappointed as she fetched fresh coffee to the table. 'Marianne is the perfect wife,' he continued, and suiting the action to the words, he slung a firm arm around her and bestowed a restrained kiss on her mouth. Restrained compared with those he had given her last night, but very nice all the same, thought Marianne, hoping wildly that it had not been given just for effect.

After breakfast, which was a rushed meal, Yves and Terry departed for the village, to the garage in Serac, roaring off in Terry's Maserati, the noise of which sent Marianne's hens back to the coop in a squawking run.

'I'm happy,' enthused Liz, a delighted grin on her expressive face. 'I can't remember being as happy as this for years. I've been thinking about it all night and I keep getting this awful feeling that it's too good to last.'

Marianne said, 'Nonsense,' in a bracing tone and wrinkled her nose at the taste of her coffee. If only she could behave in this extrovert fashion, if only she could come into a room and fling her arms around Yves!

Carefully schooling her features, she smiled into the blue eyes. 'You'll have to make it up to him, you've kept him waiting long enough.'

'I will.' Liz's voice was soft and reflective. 'I think I'll have a baby as soon as possible. It will be something to take my mind off the track when he's racing.'

Marianne tut-tutted. 'That's no reason for having a baby,' she scolded.

'And what's yours?' Liz asked sarcastically, her eyes very wide.

Marianne found herself blushing as she realised that there was no way out of the trap into which her unwary tongue had led her. 'It just happened,' she stuttered. 'There wasn't any particular reason.'

'See what I mean?' Liz was triumphant and went on smugly, 'I'm going to plan things properly, none of this hit or miss business for me.'

Marianne rose from the table, suddenly feeling very ill. She had hardly eaten anything and the coffee tasted foul. There was a knot of nausea in her stomach and she felt giddy. With a muttered excuse she fled to the downstairs cloakroom and spent a vile fifteen minutes alternately retching and shivering while she drank cold water. During this time she went over in her mind everything she had eaten for the past twenty-four hours.

Everything had been quite innocuous. Good, plain home cooking, they hadn't had a meal out. Nobody else showed signs of being ill; maybe she had 'flu coming on. She groaned with despair. Of all the times when she could have been ill—to start now with two guests in the house! Her hands clasped the rim of the porcelain basin tightly as she fought down another bout of nausea, then Sylvie came to put an arm around her and lead her back to the kitchen.

'Please sit down, *madame*,' her young face was touched by a comical concern. 'I will fetch you a little cognac, you are very pale and your hands are freezing.' Busily, she pushed Marianne back on to a chair. 'Perhaps it would be better if you made yourself comfortable in bed?' she suggested.

'I'm all right.' Marianne turned a white face on Liz, who was hovering. 'Don't look so concerned,' she spoke sharply. 'There's nothing the matter with me. I've probably eaten something, although I can't think what. I've been feeling a bit off colour since breakfast.'

'If this is what you're like when you're a *bit* off colour, heaven help us when you're really ill,' Liz scolded. 'Here, take this,' she thrust a glass of cognac into Marianne's cold fingers. 'Stop shivering,' Liz soothed. 'You deserve to be ill, behaving as you're doing now. As for suggesting it's something you've eaten or 'flu, don't be so stupid. I come from a large family and I think I recognise the symptoms. Haven't you ever heard of morning sickness? That's all that's wrong with you.' She was so briskly hardheaded that it sent a warm glow through Marianne's cold body, and this, allied to the effect which the brandy had upon her, was very comforting. Slowly a little colour returned to her pale face.

Liz observed this with satisfaction as she chafed Marianne's cold fingers. 'Look, why don't you do as Sylvie suggested and go to bed for a while? Oh yes!' Liz grinned. 'I can understand enough French for that. Come on, sweetie, up with you and into bed. I'll bring you a hot water bottle.'

Reluctantly Marianne allowed herself to be hustled upstairs to the bedroom. 'Oh lord!' Liz came in carrying the hot bottles. 'Is this what the genuine French bedroom is like? All functional and utilitarian,' she sniffed in a disparaging manner. 'Not a frill anywhere! I'm glad they do them better than this in hotels.' She looked around and gave a mock shiver. 'Myself, I'd find all this white and starch absolute death to romance. Aren't you going to change it, tart it up a bit?'

This was very like the remark Yves had made the previous evening, and Marianne found herself looking around the room with new eyes. They were both right, Yves and Liz. The room did not even look comfortable. Like Grand'mère's room, it was just a place to sleep. It had no personality.

'We'll go and buy frilly covers for everything,' she promised. 'Just as soon as we can.'

'And some nice cheerful rugs.' Liz was becoming enthusiastic. 'I can see it. A sandy colour for the walls—you can keep the white paint. A striking picture for the wall opposite the window—Sunflowers, by that man who cut his ear off. Covers in old gold, a coffee-coloured carpet, cream and brown shaggy rugs, it would look much better. Why don't you move in to the big room next door for a while and have this one done out properly?'

Marianne snuggled down with the bottles under the soft plumeau. 'Call me when the men get back,' she directed, 'and don't you dare say a word, not to Yves anyway. He doesn't know yet and he'd only start fussing. Tell him I'm all right, it's just a bit of a headache.' She closed her eyes; the hot bottles were a great comfort and everything faded from her mind in a haze of warmth. Perhaps she had been doing too much, as Yves had said. She would take things a little easier from now on.

A stealthy movement at the side of the bed roused her and she opened her eyes to find Yves standing there, looking down at her with an odd expression on his face—a mixture of concern and anger. At once she was alert.

'Have they towed off Liz's car?'

'Yes,' he frowned. 'Liz says that you have a headache and have been ill. Shall I send for the doctor?'

'Certainly not!' Marianne sat up. 'I'm fine now.' As she said it, she realised that she did feel extremely well.

'Then will you explain why I find you in bed, looking like a small ghost?'

'I was very sick and I had an awful headache, it was Liz and Sylvie who sent me to bed.' Marianne sounded mutinous.

His grey eyes glittered down at her and she shrank from the anger in their depths. 'You were worrying about that car,' his face was grim. 'It was an ordinary brake failure, a seal went in the master cylinder, so you see, you had no need to worry, or is it that you still do not trust me?'

The challenge brought Marianne upright in bed. 'Of course I trust you,' she snapped the words off sharply, 'but I can't help worring, can I? I'm a worrier by nature and I can't stop to order.' She raised indignant eyes to his. 'I have to put up with you doing your strong, silent man thing, so you'll just have to accept that when problems arise, I'm going to worry about them until they're gone.'

'Could you not try sharing them, these problems about which you agonise? If you did that, would it not be better?' The angry gleam had gone from his eyes and his mouth had lost its hard line. Almost it seemed that he was pleading with her and she raised her eyes, a puzzled look in their greeny-grey depths.

'Idiot,' she said huskily. 'What's the use of both of us worrying? One of us should remain composed, surely? I'll leave all the action to you and I'll sit at home and chew my fingernails.' With this, she swung herself to her feet and scrabbled around for the sandals which she had dropped by the side of the bed. 'Come on,' she continued briskly. 'I've wasted enough time this morning already and I'm starving!' At the door she paused and looked back. 'You and Liz were quite right,' her gaze took in the thick white bedspread carefully folded back, the stark white walls and the too tidy atmosphere. 'This room wants cheering up.'

Yves turned with her, looking over her shoulder, his hand heavy about her waist. 'It is sufficient for a bachelor,' there was a wry twist to his mouth, 'but a married man should have something better than this. Why do we not get the bigger room next door redecorated and refurnished? It would be more comfortable than this one.'

'That's Grand'mère's room!' She spoke without thinking.

'So!' he raised an eyebrow. 'And is Grand'mère using it? Grand'mère is dead, Marianne. Turn your talents on that room and let us see what you can make of it, but you will not do it yourself! We will have Marcel out from Rémy for that and while he is decorating it we will shop for new furniture and carpets.'

That evening Terry declared himself sufficiently rested to attempt the long drive to Calais. He preferred to travel at night, as there was less traffic on the roads, and he and a tearful but smiling Liz departed in the muted roar of a powerful engine.

'Promise to write,' Liz screamed above the roar of the exhaust. 'I'll tell you when and where so you can send a card!' Liz had opted for a quiet wedding. 'I've had one with all the trimmings,' she had explained. 'Quite exhausting, I assure you. Hundreds of people all in their Sunday-go-to-meeting clothes, I felt like nothing on earth when it was all over. This one's going to be quiet and cosy, just Terry and me and a bloke in the Registrar's Office. That's why I'm not inviting you or anybody else, but we'll call in when we're this way—April, I think. You'll be a fair size by then and your sexy hunk will be all protective and proud. Have you told him yet?'

Marianne had shaken her head and Liz had giggled. 'You won't be able to keep it a secret much longer,' she had jeered. 'I think I could spot the difference in you now, so he's bound to notice soon. Those eyes of his!' Liz gave a dramatic shudder. 'They don't miss much, do they?'

Now Liz was gone and the house seemed too quiet. Marianne found herself missing the blunt comments and the caustic wit of her friend. As if he knew that she would miss her friend for a while, Yves kept his outside work to a minimum and spent more time with her in the office.

Marcel came from Rémy in a plain van which, when opened, disgorged several stepladders, a quantity of paint, rolls of paper and some new louvred shutters which were to be fixed to the inside of the windows. Marianne surveyed these last items with deep satisfaction. Now when the hot weather came, the windows could be opened at night without anyone being blown out of bed!

Marcel also brought a helper, a young man who was, in Marianne's opinion, a bit flashy. He made her feel uncomfortable and she avoided him whenever possible. Not so Sylvie; that young lady temporarily transferred her affections from the faithful Jacques to the newcomer and Marianne worried when she found a bright-eyed, flushed Sylvie lurking behind closed doors with somebody who was evidently a fast worker, even if Marcel did not seem to think so! Marianne might have worried, but Jacques did not. He was not seen for two days and then he arrived in Marianne's Mini which, besides the overhaul, had suffered a paint job done on it, for it was now a gleaming orange colour with black stripes along the bottom of the doors, and it also sported a green fibreglass aerial which swayed a good three and half feet above the roof.

Jacques was very pleased with his car and after thanking Madame Bersac for her kindness in selling it to him, departed with a radiant Sylvie clutching his arm and talking nineteen to the dozen. The speed with which Sylvie could change her allegiance made Marianne breathless, and she mentioned it the next morning when she and Sylvie were changing the bedlinen.

Sylvie gave her a worldly-wise smile. 'But of course, *madame.*' Sylvie showed surprise that Marianne should be so naïve. 'A little uncertainty is good for a man. Jacques had begun to take me for granted, I think. It was time that he woke up and realised that he was not the only man in the world. He knows it now, so he will be more attentive.'

She turned her attention to the pile of soiled linen and began to fold sheets, stuffing them vigorously into the bag.

That night after dinner Marianne mentioned it to Yves as they sat before the fire in the salon. 'Sylvie was so . . . so old,' she explained, 'so blasée, I felt like a child beside her.'

Yves watched the smoke rising from his pipe, and through it he looked at his wife with a wry humour.

'Compared with Sylvie, you *are* a child.' He made it sound almost a compliment, and Marianne flushed. 'Sylvie was born as old as Eve,' he continued with a chuckle. 'She probably drooped her eyelids, fluttered her lashes and pouted at boys when she was in her perambulator. Not like you, my little English Miss. You were born knowing nothing, and thanks to Grand'mère, you still know nothing. You could seduce a man with no effort at all, but you wouldn't know you were doing it and you'd be frightened silly at the result.'

Marianne's eyes opened wide at this comment; she didn't know whether it was a compliment or one of his scathing remarks. 'Tell me, *monsieur*, how would I go about seducing you? Do I have to flutter my lashes and pout?' She slid her long legs from their curled up position on the couch and rearranged the graceful folds of her fine wool evening skirt.

'No,' he said almost to himself so that she could hardly hear him. 'You don't need tricks like that, *ma mie*. Did I not say that you do it unconsciously?'

Marianne was looking at him with wide eyes. Her heart was beating rather fast and she seemed to have difficulty in getting enough air to breathe. Deliberately, she leaned back against the cushions and stretched herself, pretending to stifle a yawn. Yves swore pungently in French and leaned forward in his chair, grabbing her about the waist and dragging her towards him. Her resistance was only a token thing, in fact it was no resistance at all. She collapsed bonelessly on to his knees and put up a hand, drawing his head down to hers. Through the silk of his shirt she could both hear and feel his heart beating, and then he raised his head to regard her flushed countenance through narrowed eyes.

'Devil!' he whispered. 'You did that deliberately, *madame*, and now you pay for it.' He undid the cord that secured the drawstring neckline of her blouse and pushed it from her shoulders, his mouth finding the hollow between her breasts. Marianne decided that she was behaving very badly and felt a faint regret that she had never thought of doing this before. Then the regret was lost in the hot tide which swept through her.

'*Madame*,' his voice came as a breath of sound in her ear, barely a whisper. '*Madame*, there is a time and place for everything. The time is quite obviously now, but this is not the place.'

'Mmmm.' Marianne allowed the wordless agreement to escape her lips and clung to his shoulders as he lifted her and carried her upstairs to the bedroom.

A heavy spatter of rain on the window panes woke her. It was still dark, but that was nothing to go by; it usually was dark until about nearly seven o'clock in the morning. But it must be earlier than that, Marianne reasoned. Yves was still in bed, she could feel his warm, hard body against her, and then she remembered that it was Sunday. That was one morning when he didn't get up so early.

It sounded as though it was going to be another horrible day. The wind was driving the rain hard against the windows, and with a perceptible shiver she sank back into the bed. Yves had a nice body, she mused, lean and powerful, with wide shoulders, narrow hips and a nice flat stomach. How would he react to the fact that her own stomach was going to be not so nice and very far from flat? He might even be angry about it, although she didn't see how he could be.

As she stirred, the by now familiar nausea struck her and she groaned. How long did this go on, she wondered, and wished she had someone she could ask. Tante Monique? Marianne shuddered. Never! Madame Berthilot? No! There was nobody else to whom she would talk about this new life growing within her. Slowly, so as not to disturb her sleeping husband, she began to slide out of the bed, intent on getting to the bathroom as quickly as possible. A hard, firm arm clamped closely about her and stopped any further movement.

Yves wasn't awake—she peeped at his sleeping face. The tightening arm about her was an unconscious reaction. That might be a good sign, she thought. Asleep, when he was without his protective coating of cynicism, he wanted her close to him. She thought about it for a few moments until the nausea came again and she knew she must move. With a determined effort she escaped from the bed and gathering up slippers and dressing gown hurried off to the bathroom, the bitterness of bile at the back of her throat.

Yves found her there fifteen minutes later, shivering and pale.

'Stupid!' he ground out the word. 'Why couldn't you say you were ill? How long have you been like this?'

'It's nothing.' She reached for the glass of water she had poured ready.

He glowered at her. 'I know what it is, Marianne. As you say, it is nothing, but it is uncomfortable while it lasts.'

She raised a still pale face and her eyes sparked green. 'You know?' Surprise made her voice quite shrill. 'Damn Liz and that doctor! I might have known they'd tell on me.' Yves was laughing and the laughter seemed to bounce off the wall tiles and echo round the bathroom. The sound of it made her irritable.

'Do share the joke,' she spat at him through clenched teeth, her voice heavy with sarcasm. 'I could do with something to laugh at. Or is the joke on me?'

'No joke!' He sobered almost at once. 'Liz did not, as you say, "tell on you", neither did the doctor. I am a farmer and I can count. I do not need anyone to tell me when my wife is with child. This sickness will last about two months, after that you will feel much better.'

Marianne surveyed him with deep dislike. Now that the need for secrecy no longer existed, she was filled with belligerence.

'Two months? Big deal! I'll be dead before then . . .!' He picked her up and carried her back to the bedroom, putting her down gently on the bed.

'No, you will not be dead, little mother. A little less shapely, perhaps, but not dead. Doesn't it please you, this coming child, or is it that you thought it was a secret? When were you going to tell me?' He chuckled. 'Oh, Marianne! Didn't I tell you some time ago that I do not tell unnecessary lies?'

'Do you mean,' she raged, 'that when you told Sylvie, you *knew*?'

'But of course.' He sounded smug.

'You mean,' she said awfully, 'that these last weeks I've been tottering around in the mornings, feeling like death but putting a brave face on it, and all the time you knew? Yves Bersac, if I had something heavy, like a hammer, I'd beat you to death and enjoy every moment of it!'

'Good, you are feeling better,' he smiled down at her. 'Would you like some coffee?'

'I'm going to have a bath,' she said with relish. 'A lovely long bath.'

'But not too hot, madame wife. Hot baths are not thought to be good for expectant mothers.' He spoke with exaggerated courtesy.

Marianne slid off the bed and walked past him with her nose in the air.

Her nose remained in its elevated position and she wore

her charming, secretarial smile, speaking only when spoken to until Sylvie bounced in. The girl's gay and uncomplicated '*Bonjour, madame, monsieur,*' filled Marianne's whole being with unutterable despair. Why couldn't she, Marianne, be gay and uncomplicated? Why couldn't she learn to ignore Yves's biting remarks, his sarcasm, his moods? She felt green with envy.

Yves broke in on her thoughts as he spoke to Sylvie.

'Tomorrow, Sylvie, Madame and I go to Rémy or to Clermont-Ferrand. We wish to purchase new furniture and carpets for the bedrooms. Now that Marcel has decorated one of them, we find the old furnishings need to be replaced with something lighter, more to Madame's taste.'

Sylvie stood hesitant, her hands clasped tightly together and her eyes fixed unwaveringly on Marianne. Yves smiled briefly at the girl and turned to his wife,

'I feel sure that you will only be too pleased to give Sylvie such articles of furniture as you no longer need. There is a quantity of small stuff in the attics also, some of which may be suitable for Sylvie.' He flashed another glance and a kind smile at the girl, who remained with her apprehensive gaze firmly fixed on Marianne.

Why can't he smile at me like that? Marianne wailed silently to herself. Yves touched her hand and brought her back from her painful envy. 'Sylvie and Jacques hope to marry soon and I have offered them the small cottage at the bottom of the hill.' Sylvie received another smile, one for which Marianne would gladly have given her back teeth. Yves continued, 'But as you know, *ma mie*, Jacques has spent part of their savings on the Mini, with Sylvie's complete consent, of course, and they do not have sufficient left to buy all the furniture they need. To start saving again would mean that their wedding would have to be delayed still further.'

Marianne smiled, a real smile, genuine and happy, 'But of course. There are any number of things upstairs which

Sylvie can have.' She turned to the girl. 'I'm so pleased—when is the wedding?'

Sylvie lost her look of apprehension. 'In about a month, *madame*. You will come, I hope? It will not be very grand, but it will be a pretty wedding, I think.'

Marianne assured her that nothing would be permitted to prevent either herself or Monsieur Yves from coming to what she was sure would be the loveliest wedding of the year, and certainly the one where the bride would be attired in the most beautiful clothes.

Sylvie nodded. Her mother, she disclosed, had obtained the pattern for the wedding dress from Paris itself and the material was from a well-known warehouse in Lyons, where only the finest silks were found. The dress had been a long time in the making and it was of great beauty, far superior to anything that could be bought. Sylvie described it in detail and then went out to feed Marianne's hens with the latest pop song on her lips.

'Thank you, Marianne,' Yves chuckled after the departing Sylvie, and then became serious. 'Jacques is a good worker, but if we did not ease their way a little, it is possible that he would seek employment in one of the new factories that are springing up around Clermont and many of the bigger towns and I should lose him. So many of the young ones have gone that way from the village. If it continues, Serac will die.' There was an expression of sadness on his face and Marianne controlled, with difficulty, a desire to put her arms around him and comfort him.

'It's the same in England,' she told him. 'Agricultural workers are leaving the farms and going to work in factories, sometimes just for the money and sometimes because of the new farming processes which have cut down on the number of men required, and the villages are emptying. What makes it worse, though, is that the village cottages are being bought up by wealthier people from the cities as weekend homes. So the price of them goes sky-high and even if a young couple wanted to stay in their village, they couldn't afford to buy their own home. It's dreadful to see whole villages without a single child in them, just old people and empty cottages that have been converted to ranch-style weekend homes.'

'Such gloomy thoughts,' Yves teased. 'Don't look so sad, madame wife. We cannot change the world. The best we can do is to make a small gesture and be content with that.'

Monday morning dawned wet and cold. Marianne went to the bedroom window and shuddered. Rain mixed with sleet was falling from a leaden sky and there was no break in the cloud. Bare branches of trees looked black against the grey background and the whole landscape looked sodden and miserable. But today they were going to Rémy or Clermont; she cheered up at the thought and hoped that it would be Clermont. It was a much longer drive and that would mean that she would have more time with Yves. They couldn't quarrel all the time, surely? She rifled through the wardrobe in search of warm clothing and as she closed the heavy oak door with a bang, she surveyed the monstrous piece of furniture with a deep dislike. She had not disliked it so much before, but now her mind was running on dainty, white closets with gold handles or perhaps golden pine where the knots in the wood had mellowed to a deep russet colour.

On her way back from the bathroom she peeped into what had been Grand'mère's room. It didn't look the same place at all. The bare white walls were now covered with a pale sand-coloured paper and she stood for a moment, visualising the carpet they would buy today. A darker gold, perhaps? Or a moss green? Green was a nice restful colour and it went with her hair. Hastily she darted back into the bedroom to dress as she heard Sylvie's light voice and the deeper rumble of Yves as he answered some question. Halfway down the stairs, she half decided on mahogany. The white and gold stuff would be lovely in the smaller room, but she couldn't see Yves being at home with it.

As she had expected, there was nothing she fancied in Rémy, so they went on to Clermont, where they spent a very pleasant afternoon wandering around furniture stores and warehouses while Marianne made up her mind about carpets, curtains and bedroom furniture. She raised her eyebrows at some of the prices, but the quality was extremely high and the workmanship was good, so that she was very well satisfied with her buys.

Having Yves with her was a great advantage. She stood him by several bedroom suites and finally chose one built on classic lines in a lovely rosy brown mahogany. There was lots of white and gold furniture and she loved it, it made her think of Versailles and the Petit Trianon, but it didn't suit a provincial farmhouse. It needed a chateau at least to show it off properly, and La Barrière was no chateau. Yves approved of the mahogany, so although the price was extremely high, they bought it. Marianne consoled herself for the massive expenditure with the thought that it was all going to last a very long time.

Ludo, who had been left behind to keep Sylvie company, gave them a vociferous welcome on their return. Sylvie had banished him to the yard while she cleaned and he had suffered the indignity in a fatalistic manner, but now he could get into the kitchen and take up his rightful place, which was under Marianne's chair, on the rug by the fire.

Marianne surveyed Sylvie's preparations for dinner and declared them to be adequate, in fact, there was nothing much for her to do. All the fires had been lit and even the dining room table had been laid, so Marianne took herself off to the bathroom and indulged in the luxury of a long, warm soak before dressing for dinner in a long velvet skirt in pine green with a paler green silk blouse. She brushed her hair into a smooth chignon, applied the minimum of make-up and went downstairs to the kitchen to cover herself with her voluminous white apron before attending to the final stages of the dinner.

She was just turning the vegetables into their respective dishes when the sound of a car turning into the yard heralded the arrival of visitors. Peeping through the kitchen window, she could just make out the shape of Bernard's van.

She let out a small squeal of despair and swore under her breath. Foiled again! She had been looking forward to a quiet evening with Yves, a time to talk about the baby and other intimate subjects, and what chance would she have now? Bernard would claim Yves's attention all the evening and half the night, and she would have to suffer the barrage of Tante Monique's questions. Hastily she counted cutlets and rapidly assessed the contents of the vegetable dishes for quantity.

Breathing a sigh of relief that there was sufficient for their unexpected guests, she discarded the apron and smoothed her hair, brushed a few imaginary specks from her long green skirt, put Ludo in the pantry, put on her best hostess smile and went forth to greet her insensitive, insufferable visitors.

With half an eye she registered that her hair was smooth and had a healthy shine and that there was colour in her cheeks; farther than that she could not go in the small mirror on the wall by the kitchen door. Her welcome for Tante Monique was quiet and restrained, accompanied by the sort of smile which she had cultivated in her business life, a pleasant, impersonal expression which soothed.

'We are delighted to hear your news.' Tante Monique, who was anything but delighted, made the remark in an unmusical voice and then spoilt the effect by saying, 'It would have been so much better, though, if we did not have to rely for our information on Madame Berthilot and that child Sylvie. A lack of communication between members of a family is always a bad thing, do you not agree?'

Marianne surveyed the short, dumpy figure of Yves's aunt and noted idly that she was wearing her favourite purple toque; that the colour did not suit her high-complexioned face and that the little sharp black eyes were darting everywhere. Marianne smiled placatingly and murmured without saying anything, another useful trick which she had learned. She kept her smile going while she returned to the kitchen to put the dishes to keep hot on the burnished top of the old range.

By eight o'clock, her smile had become so rigid that she feared her face would crack. Bernard did not appear to want to closet himself with Yves in the office, so Marianne, glad to have something to do to take her away from the older woman's heavy-handed innuendoes, started to set extra places while Yves dispensed sherry for the ladies and Ricard for Bernard and himself.

Going in to call them for dinner, Marianne found that Yves had retreated into a taciturn silence while Bernard was dutifully echoing each and every one of his mother's dictums. Presently it became clear to Marianne that Tante had come with an axe to grind.

'I hear that you are giving away unwanted furniture from La Barrière. Giving it to Sylvie Berthilot!' Tante's tones were suitably shocked. Marianne murmured again without saying anything. 'I am amazed, not only amazed but outraged!' Tante allowed her voice to rise in protest.

'Why?' Yves was not even bothering to be polite.

Tante turned to him. 'I do not expect any family feeling from your wife, nephew, how could she have any when she has never had a family, but from you, I expected better treatment than this. As I am a daughter of a younger brother of your grandfather, surely you should have considered me first when you are so munificently giving away what very well might be family heirlooms.'

Tante followed this up with a short lecture on the extravagance of the modern housewife, who changed her carpets as often as she changed her clothes and did not realise the value of money kept in the bank.

Marianne first raised her eyebrows and then closed her eyes. Before her closed lids swam a vision of the house next to the butcher's shop, an ugly house which bulged from cellar to attics with Tante Monique's prized possessions. There was no corner of any room that did not contain something. Tables and cabinets supported framed photographs by the hundred and a shop could be stocked with figurines and ornaments and there would still have been a surplus in the house. It was literally stuffed full!

Marianne opened her mouth to speak, but was forestalled by the older woman, who gave a short homily on the wisdom of placing valuable antique furniture in the hands of somebody who would know how to take care of it. Somebody quite unlike the modern generation, who would chop up priceless treasures for firewood as soon as they had enough money to buy the plastic modern furnishings which could be wiped clean with a damp cloth and never needed polishing.

Marianne's head had started to ache and she found it wwwasbecomingincreasinglydifficulttokeephertemper.She glanced at Yves, a pleading look in her eyes. As if he had been waiting for this signal, he interrupted his aunt's monologue.

'I have told Jacques and Sylvie that they may have such pieces as they require.' He sounded bored and indifferent, but there was a fiendish look in his eyes. 'There are, however,' he continued with every appearance of willingness to help, 'several very large wardrobes and other items which are too big for the small cottage in which they are going to live.' Behind the drooping lids, his eyes seemed to be full of an unholy satisfaction and she was almost certain that he winked at her, 'I will have these pieces sent down to your house.' Yves was bland but firm. 'The men will place them wherever you wish them to go. Fortunately, no antiques are involved, the pieces are of good quality but quite hideous and are worth very little. Such valuable items as there are at La Barrière are being cared for and will not be disposed of.'

He rose from his chair and looked sternly at Marianne, who was having difficulty in choking back hysterical giggles at the thought of Tante Monique attempting to find room for two vast glass-fronted wardrobes and several equally vast chests of drawers, not to mention a collection of iron bedsteads, gilded to look like brass, and several large gloomy-looking religious pictures.

'I think, *madame*, that we have delayed dinner long enough.' Yves's expression dared her to deny it. 'Marianne is a very good cook,' this was to his aunt, who sniffed disparagingly. 'We insult my wife by allowing her dinner to spoil,' and without waiting, he grasped his aunt's arm and drew her firmly out of the room.

CHAPTER TEN

DINNER came to an end at last and Marianne breathed a sigh of relief. The whole long process had worn her nerves very thin. She wished momentarily that they were in England where meals took up far less time. A glance at her wristwatch told her that it was past ten o'clock, and Bernard was still occupied in giving Yves the names of several wines which he was sure were better and cheaper than the ones in the cellar at La Barrière. Yves listened to him patiently, not bothering to dispute his cousin's opinions.

Marianne rose in a determined way and went to the kitchen where the coffee pot was gurgling on the range.

After piling cups, saucers, sugar and cream on the tray, she deftly removed the filter from the pot and replaced it with the lid before carrying her loaded tray into the dining room. Yves had brought the cognac and glasses earlier and she set these in front of him while she busied herself with the coffee cups.

'You make good coffee.' Tante Monique disturbed her train of thought and she looked up and smiled sweetly at the older woman.

'My friend brought me this coffee from England.' She dripped honey with the words. 'It's Blue Mountain—Jamaican, I think. There's no chicory in it.' Unwittingly she had made the opening which her visitors had been waiting for.

'The English lady,' Bernard said it so innocently! 'We were relieved to hear that she was not hurt too badly in the crash, as we were at your own good fortune. You had a miraculous escape, truly miraculous! Others have not been so fortunate,' he added unctuously.

'Yes, we were lucky.' Marianne kept her voice cool and banished every trace of emotion from her face except that of polite uninterest. She noticed that the coffee which she was pouring into Yves's cup fell in a steady stream. That was good, it showed that her hands were steady. 'And so fortunate, as you said.' Her voice smoothed out to a purr. 'Just imagine the gossip if we had been badly hurt or maybe killed. The good people of Serac would have held up their hands in horror. Both of Yves's wives in the same sort of accident in the same place! I expect they chattered about it enough as it is.' Her pale auburn hair was crackling and each individual hair was standing away from her scalp.

'It was an accident.' Bernard made the statement sound more like an accusation. Marianne flashed a look at Yves from under her lashes. He was calmly drinking his coffee and watching the smoke rise from the cigar he was smoking. It rose in a pale blue column, straight upwards in the still air of the room. That's two of us with good nerves, she thought, and smiled at him.

'We heard that the car had been examined most closely,' Bernard was digging at a sore point, 'first by Henri at the garage and later by an Englishman. Of course, the police examined it as well.' He turned to his mother. 'That is so, is it not, Maman?' It was such an innocent thing to say and he said it so innocently!

Tante Monique nodded vigorously, her purple toque slipping sideways so that she had to put up a hand to straighten it. 'That is so, *mon fils*. I myself saw the gendarmerie in the garage examining the car. I would not have noticed, but they left their motorcycles outside and I saw them. Naturally, one is curious.' Marianne swung round to face the older woman. 'Yes, you *would* be curious,' she said under her breath.

'Why should the police examine the car?' Yves demanded coldly. 'Or did somebody go bleating to them about coincidences?' He raised an eyebrow and looked at Bernard pointedly. 'Was it you, little cousin? Were you once more concerned for my wife's safety?' He smiled at Bernard, but there was no humour in the smile. Meditatively, Marianne stirred her coffee, watching the spoon making little creamy circles in the dark brown liquid.

'Gisèle died,' Tante said flatly and Yves turned to her.

'There was nothing mysterious about Gisèle's death as you should know. Had there been anything suspicious, the police would have been here asking questions.' Yves's voice was equally flat.

'You may call it an accident, nephew, but I do not.' Tante's face was becoming nearly the same colour as her hat. 'There are more ways of getting rid of an unwanted wife than one. Gisèle was driven to do what she did by you and the old woman. You will never make me believe otherwise.'

'Tante,' Yves was smiling, an unpleasant smile, 'you force me to this. I do not wish to drag up past histories, but you shall not slander my grandmother. Did you never ask yourself where Gisèle was going that afternoon?'

His aunt looked at him oddly. 'To her mother, of course, where else would she go?'

'But her mother no longer lived in Serac, don't you remember? When Gisèle married me, Madame Fabré went to La Rochelle to keep house for her widowed brother.'

'Then she was going to La Rochelle.' Tante Monique was filled with triumph.

Yves shook his head sadly. 'Without money or even a change of clothing? It is hundreds of kilometres to La Rochelle. Gisèle was not very intelligent, but she was sensible enough to provide for herself on a journey of that length. She would have needed money, if only for petrol.' Yves was being ruthless and Marianne glanced at him with surprise. These were just the things which Liz had said! But then, if Liz could work it out without having met Gisèle, why shouldn't Yves, who knew Gisèle very well?

Tante fiddled with the ornate clasp of her handbag and her colour deepened even further as Yves continued.

'Gisèle ran out of this house without even taking her purse, and what is more important, she didn't know that the old Fiat was going to be outside the yard. Jacques had left it there temporarily only a few minutes before Gisèle found it. No, *ma tante*, Gisèle was not thinking of going any distance, certainly no farther than Serac. But to whom would she go in Serac? Her mother was no longer there and she had no relatives or friends.' He paused for a second, 'Do you wish me to continue, Tante?'

Marianne idly looked up from the contemplation of her coffee cup and her eyes widened as she saw the look on Bernard's face. It was colourless and covered with a film of perspiration. She opened her mouth to say something and swiftly Yves's hand covered hers where it rested on the table top. Covered it, closed about it and squeezed warningly.

'That's what Liz said,' she burst out in English. 'Liz said she would be going to another man, and I know now who it was.' The grip on her fingers became painful.

'Be quiet, Marianne!' Yves also spoke in English, but Marianne would not be warned. She ignored the grip on her fingers, the warning pressure.

'No, I won't be quiet!' She was defiant. 'When I think about it, I see red! I'm seeing red now. The sneaky, greasy little pig!'

'Marianne!' he warned once more, but she ignored that warning as well, continuing in English—it seemed to give her a wider scope. 'He started the rumours as well, I bet. Oh, don't you see?'

'Marianne,' his voice was a quiet reproof as he answered her in English, 'of course I see and I also understand. You can't tell me anything I don't already know. I have always known. Did you think that Gisèle wouldn't have told me? She shrieked it at me at least once every day.'

'And you're going to let him get away with it?' Disbelief filled her. 'Well, he's *not* getting away with it!' She was defiant. 'And don't try to stop me, because I won't be stopped.' Fury welled up in her and she faced him with blazing eyes. A curious little look crossed his face—a look of reluctant admiration with tenderness and exasperation all mixed up in it. She turned to Bernard and reverted to French.

'Gisèle was coming to you, wasn't she, Bernard? Don't bother to deny it! But she was killed on the way. You saw your chance and took it like the little opportunist that you are. It was all right to have an affair with her up here at La Barrière, but you didn't want Serac to know, because if Serac knew, then your mother would have known as well.

When Gisèle was killed in the car, you knew that sooner or later somebody would ask that question, "Where was Gisèle going? And to whom?" It wouldn't have taken Serac long to have come up with the right answer, so you gave them something else to think about. You started those rumours about Yves.'

Marianne paused for breath while she sorted out the thoughts whirling through her head. There were an awful lot of them and she tried to get them into some semblance of order.

'That's it!' she smiled at Yves's cousin, a bright dangerous smile. 'Your mother would have thrown you out, wouldn't she? Because it's all hers—the house, the shop and the money in the bank—and respectability is her god. She wouldn't have had you under her roof. You had a lot to lose and you took a chance, spreading your slimy bits of gossip with the veal cutlets and the hundred-gramme packs of pâté, and you succeeded beyond your wildest dreams, didn't you?' Marianne rapped out the words and noted that Tante's face was a brick red colour by now and that she was weeping noisily as she implored Yves to control his wife.

'An impossibility, Tante.' Yves gave a Gallic shrug. 'My wife does not permit of control. She has become very British. It is a difference in outlook between two nations. In England, men do not control their wives, they humour them.'

Tante Monique turned back to Marianne, sobbing gustily.

'Have you no feeling, *madame*, for a mother's heart, that you should say such things of my son? Where are your facts? All this is supposition. To accuse him without evidence, to brand him, to suggest that he and Gisèle. . . .'

'Look at his face,' Marianne turned to the older woman. 'Look at it! He's sweating with fear,' scornfully, she turned a green gaze on Bernard. 'And what has he done to Yves,' she demanded, 'but just those things you've said? He accused Yves with no evidence, no facts, and why?' Marianne's lips were curved in a dangerous little smile, almost a snarl. 'Because he believed that Yves had done those things? No, he didn't even have that excuse. He spread the rumours to keep his own precious reputation clean. To keep him snug and well fed while another man had to suffer.' She turned back to Bernard's mother. 'What would you have said, Tante, if Gisèle had turned up on your doorstep and told you that she had left her husband and had come to seek shelter with her lover? No, don't tell me, I know what you would have done. You'd have turned her off and turned Bernard out. You've never let him have anything of his own! Bernard knew what you would do as well. That's why he had to dirty another man to keep his own fat little self clean.'

Suddenly Marianne felt desperately tired, she wanted to weep with tiredness. She sat down in her chair quickly and with a hand that was, by now, very unsteady, and poured herself a fresh cup of coffee. Yves came to stand behind her chair, his hands heavy on her shoulders. She tilted her head back to look at him and felt the coffee reviving her, a warm, sweet stream that gave her new life.

'You have finished, Marianne?' The question came softly and she glared up at him.

'No, I haven't damn well finished.' His gentle question had stirred her back into life and from feeling tired, she became belligerent. 'I know that I've upset everybody and I'm not sorry, not one little bit. I don't think I'd care if I never saw your relations again. In fact, if they dropped dead here on the dining room floor, I'd do a dance! When I think you've had to put up with all this for years, I want to strangle them!' She pushed back her chair and stood up. 'I'd like them to go.' Her brief spurt of anger was evaporating fast. 'They make me sick, both of them. Get them out of my sight, they offend me!' She found that she was beginning to shiver uncontrollably and held on tightly to the back of her chair. 'There's a bad smell in this room, Yves— will you let in some fresh air, please?'

Yves looked at his wife with what could very well have been amusement, but Marianne was past analysing expressions. She didn't care any more if he was amused or in a tearing temper, all she wanted to do was to get away somewhere quiet and have a long satisfying cry.

Yves paused with his hands on the curtains. 'It is raining, *chérie*,' he murmured, 'the curtains will get wet.'

'Then I'll go upstairs,' she retorted. 'It will be fresher up there. I can't tolerate this room any longer. The smell of dung is sweeter!'

At the doorway she paused with her hand on the knob, turning to fire off her last shots. Her eyes glittered green again as she eyed her husband's relatives with acute disfavour. 'What I've said here tonight, I've said between the four of us, and it will never be heard again unless I hear some more of Bernard's filthy little rumours. If you want to start any more tongues wagging, you can tell them that I'm a harpy and that my husband can't control me. Tell them that eight years in England have turned me into a termagant. That should make a fine sauce to go with your meat, Bernard. Oh!' Tiredness swept over her again and this time it was not to be denied. 'Tell them what you like, but get out of this house!' Carefully and with great violence, she slammed the door behind her.

In the newly decorated bedroom she paused, her eyes coming to rest on the low nursing chair by the window. She and Sylvie had found it in one of the attics and had dragged it down to be scrubbed and polished before setting it where it now stood. There was no other furniture in the room, it stood silent and empty awaiting the new carpet and furniture which she and Yves had chosen that afternoon in Clermont.

Had it been only that afternoon? It seemed like a

hundred years since she had made Yves stand by the mahogany bedroom suite, to see if it suited him, and they had argued amicably over the colour of the carpet. Marianne dragged herself back to the bedroom which they were occupying and methodically undressed herself, shrugging her shoulders into her robe before crossing to the bathroom.

The water in the cold tap was icy and she shivered as she splashed it on her face, removing her make-up. Lifting her head, she caught a glimpse of herself in the mirror and stared with horror at the white face that stared back at her. She looked wild, like one of the furies from an old Greek play, and try as she would, her features would not reassemble themselves into their usual impersonality.

Despairingly, she went back to the empty, redecorated bedroom and seated herself in the little nursing chair. There was nothing to look at through the window, only the blackness of the night; there was no moon and thick cloud covered the sky, shutting out the stars. She heard vaguely the sound of their guests leaving, the slam of the door, the chatter of Bernard's van as he started the engine, and idly she watched the headlights as first they illuminated the open gate of the yard and then swung round to point downhill.

She felt numb, almost incapable of thought except to be remotely pleased that there would be no more tales about Yves in Serac. He was going to be quite furious, of that she was certain. He had tried to stop her and she had refused to be stopped. Her behaviour had been disgusting; she was disgusted with herself. She gave a little sob and the tears began to fall. She let them flow down her cheeks unheeded.

Gradually the numbness wore off and the pain started to make itself felt. What had she done? There might be no more tales of Gisèle's death, but was that going to help her? She didn't think so. She recalled the way Yves had dissociated himself from her. What was it he had said? The words came back to her and she shuddered. 'My wife does not permit of control.' She cringed back in the chair. If only she had listened to him when he had said 'enough', but she hadn't! She had been far too ready with her tongue and she had let it wag without restraint.

She listened for his footstep on the stair, but the old house was silent. He probably never wanted to see her again, and if he did—She pictured his face filled with revulsion and a little moan escaped her. Madame Bersac, she thought. Well, she wouldn't be Madame Bersac for much longer. The idea that Yves would never forgive her became firmly rooted in her brain. He would hate her; she hated herself!

For how long she sat there, she didn't know. All she could think about was that any hopes she had had were smashed, ruined beyond repair. What man could ever love, even feel the smallest spark of affection for a woman who had behaved as she had done?

She could leave, of course. Leave Yves and this house, leave France—but that would be running away, and there was the baby to consider. No! She shook her head. She had made her bed last October when she had married him and if the bed was uncomfortable, it was because she had made it so herself, in a spasm of ungovernable rage.

With a start, she realised that Yves was beside her. She hadn't heard him come up the stairs, but there he was, looking out of the window into the rain-soaked darkness. Some small regret touched her.

'I'm sorry, Yves,' she whispered. 'Not sorry about what I said or how I said it, but perhaps about what they'll make of it. Have I made it worse for you? I didn't intend to. It was just that I lost my temper—I don't do it often.' She could hear herself chattering and she shut her mouth firmly.

He wouldn't send her away, she was suddenly quite sure about that. Whatever she had done, he wouldn't tell her to go. He wasn't mean or petty, they had made a contract and he would no more break his side of it than she would break hers. She sat quite still in the chair, her robe wound tightly about her and her hair in a flood around her shoulders. Her arms felt empty and she raised them, looking at him in the darkness with an expression of regret.

With a muffled sound Yves dropped on his knees beside her and leaning forward, buried his face in the warmth of her breast. Without conscious volition her arms went about his shoulders, one hand lifting to press his head closer against her while her fingers stroked his thick black hair. So black! She watched the strands as they slid through her hands, so soft, so dear, and a wry smile touched her face.

Go away? Leave him? Not unless he threw her out, bag and baggage and he would not do that. He might not love her, but he wanted her, and she would make that enough. It wouldn't satisfy her, but it would be better than nothing and she would keep her integrity because Yves would never pretend to an emotion he didn't feel, neither would he make her any false promises. It would do, it would *have* to do, for it was all she would get, and as she had told herself before, it was better than nothing.

Weak, pale sunlight touched her face, rousing her. Some time during the night Yves must have carried her into the other bedroom and put her into bed. She lay in it now, warm and peaceful. She tried to remember all the noble thoughts which had passed through her mind before she had fallen asleep in the chair. She was very pleased with them and she turned to contemplate her husband. His eyes were open and he was contemplating her with an unfamiliar gentleness.

'Good morning, *chérie*. So you slept at last.' Marianne nodded dumbly, some part of her forgetting all her noble thoughts. It was amazing what a night's sleep and a little sunshine could do!

'I'm sorry,' she mumbled. 'Last night I behaved very badly. You would be quite justified in throwing me out. I don't know how I looked or how I sounded, but it must have been terrible. Like a virago! It was wrong of me, and especially as it was to guests, no matter how unwelcome I found them.'

'You rent them, tooth and nail.' A smile curved his well shaped mouth. 'You were quite magnificent, a snarling, spitting but very dignified cat. Even your snarls were aristocratic. Poor Tante and Bernard, I felt sorry for them. They weren't expecting anything like that. They thought you were still the Marianne of the old days, the quiet, easily led girl who stood beside Grand'mère and who was gentle and respectful.'

Marianne allowed her surprise to show. 'You weren't disgusted?' She looked at him closely. 'You sat there so silently, you hardly said a word, you just looked. I know you tried to stop me and I'm sorry. No, I'm not!' she was defiant. 'I might have been sorry if either of those precious pair had shown the slightest trace of sorrow for what they did to you, but they weren't sorry at all. Bernard was only concerned that he'd been found out and Tante Monique was only concerned that Bernard hadn't been always what she thought he was.'

'Now, why should I be disgusted?' Yves smiled. 'Because my wife made a scene? I am quite used to scenes, *ma mie*. I lived with Gisèle for four years!'

'I thought you'd turn me out, or if you didn't, you'd start treating me with another dose of that icy reserve like when I first came back.'

She could feel his laughter. 'Turn you out? When I'd been plotting how to get you into bed ever since you were about sixteen?' He smiled across at her. 'Grand'mère knew what I was up to, she kept a very close eye on you and on me. I didn't get a chance.'

Marianne hardly heard him, she was still back in the previous evening, hearing herself, strident and uncontrolled.

'You aren't listening to me,' he complained. 'Are you still worried about last night? You've no need to be. The things you said needed saying. For too long, Serac has been like a stagnant pond. Foul things have been brewing under the surface. It was time that somebody stirred them up, if only to show Tante Monique the hell's brew that Bernard was concocting. I couldn't do anything, after all, I was a part of it, but you—you were somebody from outside. To be fair to Tante, I don't think she knew what Bernard was up to, and to be fair to Bernard, what was he but what his mother had made him; a little dog to run at her bidding with never a chance of a life of his own.'

Yves turned on his back and laced his fingers behind his head while Marianne looked at him with patent disbelief. Where was the sardonic, sarcastic, withdrawn Yves, the one who had called her 'Little English Miss' as if it was an insult? He turned his head to look at her.

'What is the matter now?' he asked. 'You had plenty to say for yourself last night, have you used up all the words?'

Marianne glared at him. Something he had just said at last made sense to her. 'You said you wanted to get me into bed when I was sixteen!'

'Mmm. I wanted it even more when you were twenty-five.'

'Then why were you so beastly? I came back here and you treated me as if I was something horrid. You were abominable!'

'I knew what the old lady had put in that stupid will. I didn't want you to get the idea that you *had* to marry me.'

'So you were as unpleasant as possible?'

'But everything is all right now, *ma mie*, isn't it? I have an admirable wife,' he pulled her close, 'and she loves me.'

'You flatter yourself, *monsieur*!' Marianne forced a laugh.

'Not at all.' His voice was bland, the voice of a well satisfied man. His hand came up swiftly to cover her mouth, cutting off the words hovering on her lips. 'Why won't you admit it, Marianne? Would it be so very humiliating for you to say "Yves, I love you"? You say it every night when I take you in my arms. Not aloud, of course,' he chuckled. 'Your body says it for you.'

Hot colour flooded her face and she twisted away from him, to be ruthlessly turned back again. 'You're hurting me!' she said on a gasp.

'You are hurting yourself,' he contradicted her, a thin thread of amusement running through the words.

'You aren't being fair!' Resolutely, she kept her gaze on the window, refusing to look at him.

'No, I'm not being fair,' he agreed with her. 'But have you forgotten, I don't have to be fair. I'm French, and we don't play cricket.'

'Mmm, I know.' At last she turned her face, to have it pulled down to his. She was allowed to raise it some moments later. 'What do you want from me?' She was almost crying.

'Everything, *ma mie*.'

'And in return?' Her courage came flooding back. 'What are you prepared to give, Yves Bersac?'

'Pah!' he shook her. 'You bargain like an old crone in the market place. Be yourself, Marianne, not a pale echo of Grand'mère, a permanently chaste virgin. Even though she was married, she remained that in her mind.'

'Some virgin!' She managed a laugh, although it was a bit shaky. 'Three months pregnant! And don't lie there laughing at me. For that you needed co-operation, it's one thing you couldn't manage on your own. Now tell me, what do I get for this everything you want from me?'

An hour later, she sighed and moved against him languidly, her eyes heavy and her lips slightly swollen.

'A fair exchange?' Yves murmured the question, his lips tracing the line of her collarbone.

Marianne nodded, her eyes a luminous green. It wasn't a bittersweet hell after all. From where she was lying in the curve of his arm, it looked remarkably like Paradise!